Costly Illusions

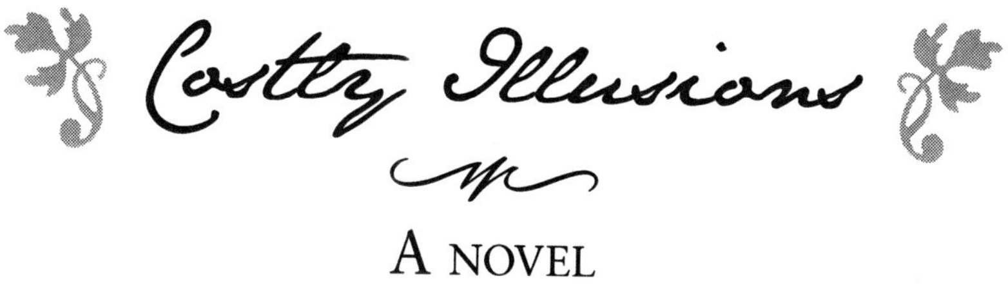

Costly Illusions

A NOVEL

Vesna Grudzinski Sutija

iUniverse, Inc.
Bloomington

COSTLY ILLUSIONS
A NOVEL

This is a work of fiction. All of the characters, names, incidents, organizations, and dialogue in this novel are either the products of the author's imagination or are used fictitiously.

iUniverse books may be ordered through booksellers or by contacting:

iUniverse
1663 Liberty Drive
Bloomington, IN 47403
www.iuniverse.com
1-800-Authors (1-800-288-4677)

Cover design:
Marin Dražančić
Cover photograph:
Marin Dražančić

ISBN: 978-1-4759-8773-7 (sc)
ISBN: 978-1-4759-8772-0 (hc)
ISBN: 978-1-4759-8771-3 (e)

Library of Congress Control Number: 2013907340

Printed in the United States of America.

iUniverse rev. date: 5/21/2013

For Erna with gratitude

Tras el vivir y el soñar
está lo que más importa:
despertar.

—Antonio Machado, *Proverbios y cantares,* LIII

Prologue

En mi soledad
he visto cósas muy claras
que no son verdad.

—Antonio Machado, *Proverbios y cantares, XVII*

Carlos, my husband of some forty years, died in July. In August I went on a trip to Venice organized by the university alumni club. The trip had been planned and paid for long before his death. It seemed unseemly to look forward to that trip with his death so recent, but our marriage was not a good one. A month of grieving mixed with memories of rare good times seemed proper, suitable. It was not so much that I grieved in the usual sense of the word. With his death I was suddenly confronted with the inevitability of life ending, pushed without warning into recognizing and acknowledging my own mortality. Even with a prolonged sickness, one is not particularly prepared for the actual end; and when it occurs, the permanence of loss is drastically, vividly acute. I went to Venice shrouded in guilty embarrassment of anticipated pleasure.

The Venice trip was great, the company enjoyable. I was part of a group of ten university professors and their spouses, also academics. The talks at mealtimes were interesting, and we argued freely about art, politics, science, and the sites we had just visited. The tour provided many organized evening events, including lectures by our group's guide, a retired general who entertained us with anecdotes from his army days and from his days as an adjunct history professor. For the most part I succeeded in pushing away my guilt about the trip. I had not had so much fun in years!

My room in a small family-run hotel was spacious, with silk wallpaper and gleaming marble floors. From the tiny balcony I could see a picture-postcard view of Venice.

From the previous night's lecture, I knew that Venice was a city that stretched across an archipelago of eighteen small islands in the marshy Venetian lagoon along the Adriatic Sea, connected by some four hundred bridges. Famous for its canals, the only roads of transportation within the city, Venice was Europe's largest car-free area. Its buildings were constructed on closely spaced wooden piles, which to my astonishment and delight were from Slovenia, Lika and Gorski Kotar in Croatia, and had thus left Velebit, a Croatian mountain, barren. Under the water the piles appeared stone-like, surprisingly intact after centuries of submersion. From my window I could see some gondolas, moving slowly and pretentiously, but the main transport was by vaporetti, the efficient and crowded water buses, and by water taxis and private boats.

This trip to Venice, so close to the country where I was

born, offered a cosmic connection, and seemed a proper place to be after a death. Its connection to Croatia, the place of my origins, would allow for a new beginning, a new chapter in my life as a widow.

The highlight of the trip was the Scarlatti concert in an old villa whose walls appeared more than five feet thick. I sat mesmerized by the music, its whimsical tunes played to crystal-clear perfection by the harpsichordist. As she later explained in the post-concert interview, she treated each Scarlatti piece as a pearl in a necklace. The concert was in the late morning, and during the intermission on the terrace, coffee was served in tiny cups, each with a thin roll of chocolate for stirring. After the concert we had lunch with the harpsichordist, an elegant woman dressed in black lace. Someone told a joke with a raunchy undertone and the harpsichordist laughed, a laugh so unexpectedly loud and with such gusto, it shattered the image of the daintily played Scarlatti pieces, as if someone had dropped the pearl necklace on the stone floor and it shattered into a thousand glittering bits.

Venice had so many museums and galleries, and I wanted to visit them all. As I visited a gallery one day, the sun shone through the glass pieces displayed on a shelf. I coveted their ruby brightness and wished I could take them home with me to recreate the Venetian sunlight on my coffee table in New York. I left the gallery and, tired of walking, stopped at a café in the Piazza San Marco. Slipping off my sandals, I wiggled my toes and counted pigeons as I looked around, sipping iced coffee.

Piazza San Marco, I read from the pages of the tourist guidebook, was paved in the twelfth century in a herringbone pattern with brick. In 1723 the bricks were replaced by dark-colored igneous rock and white Istrian stone set in a geometrical design similar to travertine—*aha,* I thought, delighted by another reference to Croatia. The design, reminiscent of Oriental rug patterns, was laid out by the architect Tirali. I also learned that the piazza was raised one meter to minimize floods. However, it was still the lowest point in Venice and the first to be flooded. The sun was bright and only a few clouds drifted in the sky. No danger of rain or floods today. I felt safe and protected within such a relaxed, unhurried existence.

I looked around, at the Doge's Palace, its gothic loggias like stone lace, so elegant in appearance, and at the basilica. Supposedly in 828 AD, two Venetian merchants stole St. Mark's remains from Alexandria and brought them to Venice by ship hidden in crates of vegetables. When the saint's body reached Venice, it was victoriously and jubilantly welcomed by the doge, who built a new church as his tomb. The symbol of St. Mark, a winged lion armed with a sword, became the city's emblem, representing strength and courage. The basilica is an enormous structure, a gothic masterpiece. Its five gigantic domes supported by the five arches breathe out a golden shimmer from its mosaics, whose tiny squares are oriented in different directions to catch and reflect the light from multiple angles. I walked inside jostled by the tourists. I craned my neck to admire the ceiling and waited patiently for the crowds to disappear so I could see the patterns on the floor.

The next day we visited the Peggy Guggenheim museum in Dorsoduro. I had promised a friend I would visit this small museum on the Grand Canal. Peggy Guggenheim, Solomon Guggenheim's niece and the wife of Max Ernst, had collected works of Picasso, Dali, Picabia, de Chirico,

Giacometti, Klee, Magritte, Brancusi, and Pollock. But the masterpieces of cubism, surrealism, and abstract expressionism were not the only reasons to go there. My friend had urged me to look at the bronze sculpture *The Angel of the City* by Marino Marini. She told me that the naked angel had a penis that was originally made removable so as not to offend any visiting dignitaries, but was eventually welded to the angel's body to prevent further thefts. I promised her a photo of the statue.

Carlos had never wanted to visit Venice. His reasons were never very clear. Something to do with decadence. I felt none of it and was overjoyed, I had decided on the trip, although it had seemed somewhat inappropriate so soon after his death.

What did I feel about Carlos's death? During his final days he was in obvious pain. As I had looked at his closed eyes and his swollen face while he lay in the hospital bed, I felt enormous pity, silently forgiving him for all the misery, real and imagined, he had caused me during our marriage. The pity was such an overpowering sentiment that it erased all other emotion, leaving my soul free of any residual anguish. And later, days after the funeral, I felt relief as I realized I was no longer a woman living on my own, separated from my husband, but a widow. Widowhood was a suitable, tolerable condition in our contemporary society. Not that I looked forward to the sympathy and compassion usually afforded a widow, but I did crave societal acceptance. It seemed that throughout my entire life I had sought acceptance, as a daughter, mother, journalist, filmmaker, scientist, and woman. With Carlos dead, and now a widow, had I finally found acceptance? I did not fully understand this persistent need to please.

Ours had not been a perfect marriage. Perfect? It hadn't even been a good marriage. In fact, for the most part it had not been a marriage at all. That was how I felt. And now I was a widow. We had never divorced, despite years of separate lives, and with his death I felt strangely free, liberated, and yet conflicted—somewhat remorseful for not being overwhelmed by sadness. Over the last several years he had called on my birthdays and our wedding anniversary, and we had visited each other. The marriage had deteriorated into a forced, unwelcome friendship. We were more than acquaintances, with too much baggage to be truly friends; our past lives our joint history. I felt an obligation to stay in touch, though it was not always sincere. Now I was out of that odd relationship and was a widow. Not a divorcee or a wife who had left her husband out of despair and unhappiness or—as he might have thought—on a whim. I had known my move and the separation were justified, but for years he had believed I would come back, like a naughty child who had committed a silly act of rebellion.

When I left Carlos, I had been truly unhappy. I had been considering leaving already, and an argument between us finally forced me to decide.

I was finishing my postdoctoral fellowship in reproductive physiology at a university lab in Caracas, Venezuela, where we lived at the time, and had a salary.

One day the strap on my sandals broke. Without much thinking I went out and bought two pairs of sandals, because I could not decide which pair I liked better. Carlos was furious.

"The strap could be repaired," he said. "You did not have to buy new sandals!"

"I work and get paid. It's my money."

"Why two pairs?

"Because I liked them both. They weren't that expensive."

"It is indulgent. We don't have money for luxuries."

"Nonsense! We are not poor. You have a good job. I have a fellowship."

"You don't need two pairs of new sandals."

"Well, just recently you bought a new Rolex watch that you did not need. But you bought it. I could have bought twenty pairs of sandals for that money!"

By that time we were both shouting.

He grabbed the front of my sweater and threw me on the bed. His hands encircled my neck, and I struggled to breathe. I tried to free myself, but the more I strained, the tighter his grip became. In panic I stopped moving and he finally let go. My sweater was torn and I had several bruises on my body and neck. My voice was hoarse for days.

That afternoon, not for the first time, I decided to leave. This time, however, it was a definite decision. I started looking for a job with deliberate purpose and a sense of freedom, born out of this long-overdue resolve to leave Carlos. When I was offered a job in New York City as a research associate and to teach an introductory course in anatomy and physiology to nursing students, I left. It had taken months to find that job, so my leaving was and was not premeditated. Carlos stayed in Caracas. Now he was dead and buried in Caracas. I was a widow in New York.

Over the years, as I was forced to change jobs and was challenged by changing circumstances, I slowly uncurled into a new person. Each challenge was a life's lesson, a reason to regroup and make an effort to mend my fractured self. I wished for the voyage to be over and done with. I wished for calm.

After the trip to Venice, my life continued in its ordinary, pedestrian stride. At my present job in the department of obstetrics and gynecology at a medical center, I prepared and gave lectures, conducted studies, analyzed data, wrote manuscripts and submitted them for publication. OB-GYN residents, my students, continued to hand papers in late and kept missing their research appointments, and I kept rescheduling them.

In the fall my son Jason came to visit me. He is tall and strong and prone to sincere bear hugs. Whenever I am enveloped, I crave to be lost in those hugs. They feel so right, and how I miss them when he goes away! There is not a day that I do not think of him in one way or other, often with prosaic concerns. Drinking tea in the morning, I wonder what he had for breakfast that day. Did he have time to read the newspaper? Probably not. He is busy. His wife is a professional, their children growing. There is probably pandemonium in their home each morning before kids leave for school. And I wished I could be there with them. I wished we lived in the same city. But we didn't. I lived alone, now leading the respectable life of a widow.

Jason was in town for a business meeting. Hugging him, I tried to share his grief over the death of his father, but mostly I felt an absence mixed with relief at my new status.

After we talked about recent events and happenings in both of our lives, Jason handed me a bunch of letters held together with a rubber band.

"Before Dad died, he gave me a safe-deposit box key and told me to destroy everything in the box. I found these letters addressed to you. I didn't destroy them. I thought you would want them. Here, take them; they're yours."

I took the letters, hesitant to look at them or at Jason. Suspecting their origin, I hastily put them away in a drawer, hiding them to avoid discussing them with Jason.

"Thanks, Jason. I will look at them later."

Changing the subject, I asked Jason about his children. Visibly relieved that we would not be discussing the letters, Jason beamed.

"Guess what? You won't believe it. Yesterday Junior beat me in chess!"

"Did you let him win?"

"No, not at all. Very ingenious checkmate." Jason smiled in disbelief. "Never dreamed ... Well ..."

Junior was my seven-year-old grandson's nickname. Jason had taught him how to play chess just the previous year. During my last visit, Junior had beaten me too. We had played several games. He won the first one in about ten minutes, the second in about twenty, and in the third, though I tried my very best, he beat me in about half an hour.

"Do you remember?" I asked Jason. "I taught you to play chess when you were about Junior's age and you played with your grandfather. It did not take long for you to beat me."

Jason smiled. "You also taught me how to play Ping-Pong, and it didn't take long for me to beat you at that either."

We had another cup of tea and chatted some more, but then Jason hugged me good-bye on his way to his business meeting and then back home.

After he left, I took the letters out of the drawer. I

looked at them more closely and took off the rubber band. I spread them out as if to count them. Then I sat down with the letters in my lap for a while, uncertain and in doubt, afraid to verify their origin. But I knew. I put the rubber band back around them and shoved them again out of sight. I closed the drawer and walked away—walked back and took them out again. No need to hide them. Jason was a mature, middle-aged man. He was married with children. I was a grandmother. When Will wrote those letters, Jason was about five years old.

Debating the best course of action, I sat there indecisive for what seemed a long time. Were they really Will's letters? Should I read them? Keep them? Destroy them? Were they real? Was I imagining them? I looked at the letters in my lap, disbelieving the touch of paper, the weight of them. Disbelieving Will wrote them. Disbelieving Will existed. Disbelieving he ever loved me. Should I read them now after all this time?

I looked at the letters again. All addressed to me, written ... I calculate mentally. Written more than thirty years ago. They are proof of Will's existence, but what else? Proof of our affair? Our love? Did he love me? He left me, and it took ten years for me to put him out of my mind, to fall out of love—ten years of my life lost while I grieved and lamented my destiny. Ten years of doubts, ten miserable years of not wanting to continue on. During that entire time I was a robot, performing daily routines, not feeling anything. Ten years while I was in my thirties, which could have been the best years of my life.

I had never thought I would get the letters back. No, that wasn't true. I had thought they did not exist. I doubted they had ever existed. Will's letters. Will's love letters to me. I thought I had imagined it all, his love and our brief time together.

But now with his letters in my hand, I felt strangely calm and in control, I told myself, "So he really did exist. I did not make him up. Here are his letters."

I began reading them, seeking assurance that once I was loved.

My dearest Alexandra,
It is late in the afternoon. I sit at my desk, planning to edit an interview, but all I see is you. I miss you so much ...

My dearest Alexandra,
I cannot believe how stupid it was of me to compliment your new boots. You were right to chide me for saying that the boots were beautiful instead of saying how lovely you looked in your new boots ...

And I remembered this. I remembered the new boots, black suede boots, and Will's compliment. And how I jokingly admonished him for seeing the boots and not me in them.

The letters were eloquent. Love on every page. Yearning, wishing we were together, wishing we would never again be apart. Yes, judging by the sentiment in these letters, I had been loved. He loved me. I felt deeply redeemed and at peace with this knowledge.

Suddenly love seemed to take up residence everywhere: in the furniture, the walls, the paintings, the flowers in a vase. As if my body, my skin, had suddenly had its capacity for sensuality restored, I felt Will's hands on me. As I kept reading the letters, I heard his voice, the voice I so loved. The evening became the night and the next morning. I kept reading.

In the morning, after I read and reread the last letter, I slowly, carefully folded the frail paper, placed the rubber band around the letters, put them in the drawer, and then closed the drawer. I gave it a small extra shove, to make sure it was closed.

The past had taken up residence in the present and altered it. I was forced to reconsider and reevaluate. This was not easy. I wondered how much of me was lost during the years of grieving over lost love, and how costly was my adjustment to Will's eventual rejection. What illusions did I sacrifice? Was it from courage or just perseverance that I shielded myself from the inevitable fragmentation of my identity? I was sure I never lost completely my sense of personal continuity, although I questioned often just how unique I was. I was convinced I never allowed my sorrow to reach the point of self-indulgence. My identity as a mother stayed intact; and my professional identity evolved and strengthened through the years of ups and downs. But I sadly concluded that my identity as a woman suffered.

At times I was conflicted about how much of it was my fault. How much of Will's decisions and choices were reactions to my behavior, and how much I was at his mercy because of his choices. From my vantage point, the way he rejected me revealed a definite character flaw. Analysis of his motives ultimately failed. It was just too painful. The easiest course of action seemed to be to forget Will ever existed, that our relationship was imagined, an illusion, a dream, not real.

Both Will and Carlos had had choices—choices that they made to my detriment. Carlos insisted on staying in a marriage no longer viable; and Will, who despite the love I now knew existed, never fought for me, never attempted a more forceful end to my marriage. Their decisions reduced my choices. If I had received Will's letters then, would I have had the courage to leave Carlos?

One

My Croatian hometown was the first free royal borough in Croatia, recognized as such by the Hungarian-Croatian king, King Andrew II, in 1209 by a document that made it the economic and military center of Croatia. The citizens have always been proud of this historical fact. Because of Turkish raids, the town was built defensively around an old fortress, constructed in the eleventh century by a prominent aristocratic family with an unpronounceable name. Over the centuries, the fortress had several owners, one of whom also built the town hall. With the arrival of Jesuits, a school and several convents were founded. The ornate baroque style of the churches and its many buildings became characteristic of the town. In the middle of the eighteenth century, it was the capital of Croatia. As the official residence of the *ban* (the viceroy), it became the residence of many Croatian noblemen as well. A fire in 1776 was so destructive, though, that the legislative and the executive institutions were moved to Zagreb.

Nobody lives in the fortress now. It is a museum filled with antique furniture, drapes, paintings, books, and documents. The fortress is surrounded by a park whose pebbled paths meander around the stone walls, spotless and unspoiled, as if they were scrubbed each morning with soap. The grass and the flowering shrubbery appear tended with utmost care. Within the greenery, wooden benches almost as old as the castle record many a love story hurriedly and haphazardly carved into their seats. The park is a popular retreat, a sanctuary and refuge from the present day's busy life and its everyday worries. People come here in the hope that the castle's calm demeanor and permanence will rub off on them, instill in them a special identity through its particular place in history.

When I was in elementary school, my friends and I often played in the park. We called the fortress *stari grad*, which means "the old castle." In winter, when covered in snow, the castle grounds were our favorite sledding site. During summer, a retired high school teacher of history gave spontaneous and improvised tours of the grounds and the museum. He particularly liked explaining things to children, and was always ready to take a group of us through the winding, ominously creaking staircases. Impeccably dressed in a suit and a bow tie, he would limp ahead of us, enthusiastically punctuating each creaking step with his cane. His explanations, though historically correct, were also amusing because he embellished them with jokes and anecdotes. Most of them included stories of his pet bird, whom he had taught to speak and sing. But what I remember best was opening a secret drawer in a magnificent cabinet decorated with inlaid mosaics and wooden curlicues.

"Alexandra, pull that drawer out," he said as he pointed to a knob on one of the cabinet's drawers.

I approached eagerly and tugged on the knob, pulling out the drawer.

"Abracadabra," he exclaimed. "Watch what happens now!" With a flourish, he pushed a hidden button on the side of the drawer. To our delight, another drawer sprang out on the opposite side of the cabinet with a distinct *ping*.

"Do it again!" we demanded.

"Abracadabra, here it goes again," he chanted, his sparse gray mustache vibrating in tempo.

Each time we were on a tour with the teacher, we made him demonstrate the secrets of that cabinet. We never tired of the *ping* of the secret drawer springing out.

After the museum tours, the teacher would wave goodbye with his cane and walk home, limping along. Left alone, we would sit in the grass, eating cherries and plump, sweet apricots from the trees in our backyards. The cherry pits turned into missiles, playfully aimed at one another's faces. Each hit was accompanied by boisterous laughter, and a miss with a desire to try again with better aim. All apricot pits were collected and saved to be cracked open with a rock and eaten later. The insides tasted like almonds.

The town hall, an impressive building dating from the sixteenth century, is the oldest town hall in Europe. During my childhood its doors were always open, but I do not remember ever going inside. I do remember some of us standing on its wide steps throwing rose petals and rice at a young just-married couple. The bride was one of my best friends, who got married right out of high school. The main square in front of the town hall has the requisite café. In the summer multicolored umbrellas shield the tables and the people drinking beer or coffee or eating ice cream. In the winter, the square is cleared of snow before any other street or sidewalks. Walking to school in the morning, we seldom crossed it, but on the way home, no longer in a hurry, we lingered in there almost every day.

The café in the main square did not have the best ice cream. The best ice cream was served in a shop owned by Ahmed, a Muslim, who came from the republic of Macedonia (not the Greek region) after the war. His daughter Zekhia, who was my age, often served ice cream in his shop. She gave us extra-large scoops and just as often, with an air of deliberate forgetfulness, did not charge. Ahmed was a large, good-natured man with unruly black hair and a drooping mustache. His boisterous laughter was the loudest, happiest laugh I had ever heard. He and his family were my father's patients, and if I happened to visit his shop while he was there, he would come out from behind the counter, energetically shake my hand, and offer me free coffee, free ice cream. Later, he would thrust a package of cream pastries into my hands.

"Alexandra," he would say, "I still owe your father for his last house call when my wife was sick. Here, here, please. Take the pastries. And say hello to your father."

Unwillingly burdened and embarrassed, I would run home, impatient to open the package.

Ahmed was not the only one who recognized me as my father's daughter. Mostly it made me uncomfortable, since I did not actually know all the people who greeted me so effusively and with various messages for my father. I tried avoiding such meetings with varying success, and later, in high school, I really hated being recognized and so easily identified. I was hardly an obedient child. In high school, after classes, my friends and I couldn't wait to be out in the streets, impatient to light our forbidden cigarettes in a place where we would not be recognized by pesky adults, who would butt into our business of being teenagers. As the daughter of one of the town's favorite physicians, I was invariably recognized and my parents were invariably informed of my transgressions.

As far as smoking went, I smoked my first cigarette the summer before second grade. Several of us, the usual group of girls and boys, had spent the summer in our dusty town and had played war games in the park of the old fortress. This was just a few years after World War II, when the war games were still the most popular entertainment. On that day, nobody wanted to play a German soldier, a very unpopular role. Everybody wanted to be a partisan, the freedom fighter. We left our make-believe weapons—tree branches—in a pile on the path leading to the street and went to my house, since it was the closest. We entered the yard, hoping for an inspiration for a new and a more challenging game.

The cherry tree had shed some leaves, so one of the older boys suggested we roll the dried ones into cigarettes. He produced matches for the game to be more authentic. Cherry-leaf cigarettes were cumbersome, and when lit they produced a wet and pungent smoke, so I had the bright idea of going into the house in search of real cigarettes. My parents did not smoke, but my mother's brother, the younger of my two maternal uncles who had his meals with us every day, did smoke, and I knew where he kept his cigarettes. With care not to alert any of the adults in the house, I sneaked into the dining room, grabbed the pack of unfiltered cigarettes, and pulled out a few to take to my friends. We lit one and took turns in smoking it.

My recollection of what happened next is hazy. I only remember that later in the afternoon, when I felt sick and had vomited, my mother was very concerned and impatiently waited for my father to come home. When he did, he tried to find out what had happened.

"Seka"—that was my nickname and meant sister—"tell me what you have eaten today. What did you have for breakfast? Did you eat anything else?"

"No, I did not. I did not eat anything. I played with my friends."

"Did anybody give you any candy, ice cream, a sandwich?"

"No, no, no. No candy, no sandwich, but I ... Oh, nothing."

Petrified of the punishment for smoking, I started to cry. My father, concerned by the vomiting, rang the mother of one of my friends to further investigate the cause of my sudden illness. He soon learned that my friend was also sick at home and had admitted to smoking a cigarette. That day was the first and the last time I saw my father furious. As he hit me once with his belt, he shouted, "Now you will really have something to cry about."

In his younger days my father's hair was dark. He wore it parted on the left side, combed and neat. His blue eyes were shaded by generous eyebrows, making his features manly, but his slightly upturned nose gave him a good-natured expression. I remember him more often with a playful smile on his face than angry or pensive. His teeth were small and his lips thin, but the general impression was of an open, attractive man. He did get angry, but whenever my sister and I misbehaved, he pleaded with us to change our ways, to improve, with sorrow in his eyes, as if he were disappointed beyond belief that his children should exhibit such unbecoming behavior.

To my regret, this expression of sadness and pity in his eyes is the one I remember most vividly. Since my father was a calm, rational, understanding person, it probably means I disappointed him more often than not.

As a doctor in postwar Yugoslavia, he was very busy and worked around the clock. During the morning he worked in a clinic. After eating lunch, the main meal of the day, he spent the afternoon in his office at home. The office had a separate entrance and a waiting room. People would wait to see him for hours. Most of them were from the surrounding villages, and they traveled to town by foot or horse carriage. Few people owned cars.

We had help in the kitchen and my mother did not always cook, but the main meal of the day was substantial, although it did not always include meat. On Sundays we had the obligatory chicken soup with homemade noodles, fried or roasted chicken, oven-roasted potatoes, and a salad from the vegetables grown in our garden. My father did not consider eating a terribly important activity. He liked desserts, anything sweet, and carried chocolate and candy in his pocket. He was a permissive parent, not demanding. My mother was demanding and inconsistent with praise or punishment—mostly punishment in my case. My father did not punish, but usually tried to explain that certain types of behavior were not acceptable and then provided alternatives.

My father loved the opera. As a medical student he earned extra money singing in the Zagreb opera choir, but at home he rarely sang. On the rare occasions when he did, it was delightful to listen to his warm baritone voice, especially to his lullabies. One of them was particularly memorable. The words were from a poem by the Russian poet Mikhail Lermontov, about a soldier home again from a battle who sings a lullaby to his son, telling him that he was safe now that his father was back. I sang the same lullaby to Jason when he was a toddler, and to my utter delight Jason sang it to his children.

My father read all kinds of books, novels as well as medical textbooks, and a variety of newspapers, sneaking the reading in between patients. There were always newspapers in our house. He read them after the midday meal if he had the time, or on Sundays when he did not see patients. We were one of the few families who had a telephone. The stupid thing rang all the time, but my father patiently answered all calls, gave advice, or went on house calls. In the evening he would ask my sister and me about school, talk about his patients, and tell us jokes. He liked company, but even though my parents were popular and were often invited to dinners or other events, they did not often entertain at home. The people who came for social visits, often without any special invitation, were served wine, plum brandy, or Turkish coffee. There was always a piece of cake or cookies to accompany the drinks. It was unthinkable not to offer refreshments to any visitors.

I do not remember when, but at some point my father became the president of the anti-alcoholic society and stopped drinking wine at home. This may have been a protective gesture, so he would not have to drink the wine he was served when he went on house calls. Our town was surrounded by vineyards, and almost everybody who was anybody had a vineyard, though they were more for weekend retreats than to produce a large quantity of wine. We did not have a vineyard. Despite his love of nature, my father did not want to cultivate a vineyard, which required too much hard work, what with weeding, spraying, pruning—every weekend. My father preferred books, chess, and music on weekends. The wine produced from the vineyards surrounding our town was almost undrinkable, although everyone thought their wine was best and bragged about each year's crop—that this wine was superior to the one from last year.

Wine was on every table, and we all started drinking rather young. At private high school parties we drank wine, never beer. There was beer, but in bars and cafés people drank white wine mixed with soda. It took some effort to get drunk on that, but even those not terribly persistent succeeded often. In any case, my father did not like or drink wine, unless it was from Dalmatia. Dalmatian wine was difficult to get in the years after the war, so becoming the president of the anti-alcoholic society gave him an opportunity to educate against excessive drinking and the excuse to refuse bad wine.

My father loved Turkish coffee and never refused a second cup. Once when I was small, I asked him what it tasted like and could I try it. He let me sip from his cup. The liquid was dark and oily and tasted very bitter. I did not like it at all and could not believe he actually drank more than a cup of this awful beverage every day! What I did not realize was that my father, who was normally very generous with sugar in his coffee, had put none into the cup of coffee he offered me.

We sometimes fought over the daily newspaper. I was

after the comics, the daily horoscope, and the crossword puzzle. During my high school years there was not a day that I did not finish the crossword puzzle. We did not have a television set. Nobody did. At the end of the fifties I saw the first television set. A group of people had gathered in front of a shop window that sold household appliances, and curious, I stopped to see what was going on. There was a television set, the very first in our town, showing a soccer game.

At home we listened to the daily news on the radio. The BBC international news was my father's favorite. We listened to soccer games, and, of course, we listened to music. Classical music and not so much the country music. But we did listen to popular music and had favorite performers. This was also music to dance to. I do not remember whether we had a gramophone. Possibly we did, because my mother was status conscious and would have considered it a must. My father was oblivious to status and could converse with anybody on any level, joking with the villagers and laughing at their crude jokes with loud enthusiasm, or arguing with his friends—and with me.

As soon as I was aware that I had opinions, I argued. I argued in school with friends and at home with my father. We argued about religion. He was not religious and never went to church. We argued about politics. He was a moderate and argued against my liberal views. When they started with Sunday Marxist seminars that I was expected to attend, he argued against my going and against Marxism in general. Whenever I argued an opposite viewpoint, he had an expression of mild disappointment. He was eloquent, rational, and calm in those discussions. And knowledgeable. He would patiently explain why he thought my arguments were insufficient and lacked conviction. I learned from these discussions, proud that he considered it important to argue with me. My mother never participated in any of our discussions, unless they were about mundane topics such as whether to practice piano, or when to go to bed, or what to have for lunch. I learned less from those discussions.

Once, an acquaintance saw me reading a romance novel published on cheap paper in weekly sections, and asked my father why he allowed me to read what he called secondhand literature. My father shrugged and said, "Why not? If she does not read this drivel, she will never be able to recognize the superiority of Tolstoy, Gogol, or Gorky." He loved the Russian authors, especially Gogol. My father was very witty and appreciated humor. When he laughed, he laughed easily and with all his heart. His patience in explaining things and his laugh are what I remember best.

I was a rebellious child. I fought constantly with my mother, and my father was forever cast in the role of referee. It was the same in regard to my sister. I thought she was spoiled and was allowed to get away with many more things than I. My parents were always asking me to be more understanding, and admonished me for not behaving according to my age. I was older and expected to be smarter, whatever that meant. My father, I felt, was more indulgent toward my sister, and I guess I was jealous. Not so much because of his attention to his younger daughter, but because he did not forgive me as easily when I misbehaved. If I was told to stay home when the yard gates were locked, I climbed over them. Not a simple feat, since they were taller than my father, who was six feet in height. I do not remember why I was so rebellious, just that my father had to calm my mother from giving me a beating with whatever was in her hand, although he could never stop her from shouting.

He was respected and liked by his patients; and later, when he was asked to head the children's clinic, a lot of children preferred him to any other doctor in town. In my early teens I got interested in track-and-field. I practiced several times a week and finally made the team. We traveled to a lot of meets out of town, and my father went on some of those trips as the team's doctor. On the trips he never coached or disciplined me or showed any particular fatherly concerns, but he was proud when the team did well. As a young man he had been an accomplished equestrian, had played tennis and skied. Actually, my parents met while skiing. He was also a good swimmer, but he never competed in any sports. He did not like anything formal, not the military, not the priests, not the police. He firmly believed that medicine was above it all. So well versed in human suffering, he possessed a natural modesty. He never bragged and could not stand bragging in others, and he immediately invented ways to make them seem ridiculous.

Often during meals he described a variety of his patients' ailments in detail and talked about medical issues, so that I had never any qualms in discussing or hearing about any bodily functions. We were urged to observe hygiene to a high degree: wash hands before eating, never share eating utensils or eat from some else's plate, and not to drink from glasses and cups that were not ours. We were forbidden to share toothbrushes, combs, and hairbrushes. But the house did not have central heating or hot running water, just cold, so the weekly bath required a concerted effort each Saturday. The water was heated in a wood-burning boiler and the bathroom could get infernally hot, which of course was nice during the winter.

In her youth, my mother was very attractive. Once I visited a friend whose mother said to me, "Your mother was a very good friend of mine before we were married. She was *very* beautiful." After a slight pause, she added, "You look like your father." I do not look like my father, although he claimed that I looked like his sister. My eyes are brown and my hair was never as dark as my father's, and it is curly. My coloring is more like my mother's, but I definitely did not inherit my upturned nose from my mother. In terms of personality traits, I probably combine some of my father's and some of my mother's. She was very concerned about material things and was forever unhappy as a doctor's wife.

When my mother first came to our town, she started a successful business in construction materials, an occupation she was expected to abandon when she married my father. After her marriage, her younger brother became the official head of the business, but my mother actually ran it from her home. Her brother ate the midday meal with us every day and stayed afterward to discuss business with my mother, his de facto boss. She missed being in the store and doing the accounting right then and there. I think she tried to turn her life into a business venture, unlike my father. Every morning during my childhood, my mother would disappear on her bicycle to buy food at the open market; and I am sure she bargained for each item, proud of her purchases. I am grateful for this gift of hers, because we never lacked anything of importance. Later, my inheritance provided me a life without worries about everyday expenses.

My mother was status conscious, but not ostentatious. When she liked a pair of shoes she would buy several pairs, often in the same color so that it seemed she wore the same shoes year in, year out. It was the same with her dresses. I remember a woolen brown dress she often wore, designed and machine knitted in a private shop. She ordered the same dress in gray and beige wool. It was a lacy affair and came in two pieces, so that she could wear a blouse underneath the woolen top. In this way she made a variety of outfits.

After the war it was not prudent to be ostentatious, and most women did not have many outfits. Most clothes were made at home. My mother did not sew. She found a woman who would come and stay with us for several weeks in our attic room, and she would produce new dresses, skirts, and blouses, and even coats. Not much ready-made clothing was available, and when it started to appear in the stores, the models were few, poorly made, and did not fit well. Having a private seamstress was relatively common, but one who stayed in your home was the ultimate luxury.

The woman my mother hired was also quite entertaining. She was extremely overweight and waddled when she walked, but she knew many jokes and kept telling my sister and me atrociously funny stories about her other clients. The story about a cheating husband whose wife emptied a pot of hot chicken soup on his paramour was well known. When told by our seamstress, it acquired fascinating new details, such as the young woman running into a nearby beauty parlor with pieces of carrots and celery in her hair, begging for a haircut and a new hairdo.

"But wait a minute, my dear," the hairdresser supposedly said. "Don't you want me to wash your hair first?"

My mother strictly forbade us to repeat such gossip, but we did anyway, embellishing it still further with jubilant curlicues of our own.

Our seamstress was never silent when she worked. If not talking, she sang songs with ingeniously funny, altered lyrics. And she was the source of all sorts of intriguing information. When a friend of mine and I kept asking her what it felt like to make love, she avoided the subject with a giggle and told us that we were too young to ask such questions—until the day she finally surrendered and told us. Her version was hilarious, and I still smile when I think of it. She became silent and looked at us with her dark eyes opened wide, and then she produced a high-pitched giggle. And another high-pitched giggle, and another, and another, until finally a long, drawn-out: "It is soooooooo gooo-o-o-o-d. Sooooooooooo gooo-ooo-ooood!" My friend and I, not really understanding, started giggling with her and repeating, "It is soooooooo gooooooood! Soooooooooo goooooooooood!" mimicking her until we were crying with laughter.

But as a seamstress, she was not very creative. I was never thrilled with her creations and wore them grudgingly, although it could have been my mother's instructions rather than her skill. When this same seamstress worked for other people, their clothes were more appealing. My mother was not especially creative in regards to clothes or cooking. They were not her priorities. Business was her priority.

We had maids, but none stayed long because my mother was too demanding. She shouted at them when they failed to produce what she expected, and she made them cry. Some were young and inexperienced, but the older, experienced ones did not stay long either.

Despite the hired help, my mother did not like to see me idle. Reading books, apart from those required as homework, was considered being idle. Whenever she saw me reading, she found something else for me to do. It was to my advantage eventually, because I learned to do many household chores without thinking, which made my life easier later in life. We grew our own vegetables, so I learned how to plant them and judge when they were ripe. We had potatoes, tomatoes, peppers, cucumbers, pumpkins, lettuce, carrots, onions, lots of strawberries, and fourteen peach trees. Peaches and strawberries were my mother's favorite fruits. When they ripened, my mother would fill baskets and have them distributed to all our friends.

The dishes she prepared were not elaborate or inventive, although she had some favorites, which by repetition became family favorites as well. Fancy ingredients were scarce and probably very expensive. We cooked what was readily available, which, to the utter astonishment of my friends in the States, included frog legs and goose liver pâté. She kept recipes for a variety of delicious cakes and pastries in an old decrepit book, which even then was falling apart, and whose pages were yellow and stained from repeated use. I am sorry I never had a chance to copy them.

Immediately after the war, the river was contaminated by the dead bodies of enemy soldiers who had been killed and dumped into the water. Or that was the explanation for the pollution. My father would not let us drink any water. Every day my mother made a thin and watery fruit compote and served that instead of drinking water. The bowl stood on a shelf in the living-dining room, and we could serve ourselves throughout the day. Its main ingredient was apples, but during the summer she would add cherries and peaches, or even plums, which were a tasty and delightful change. Lemons were expensive and hard to find, but occasionally my mother would find them and the compote would have a lemony taste. It was quite drinkable, never too sweet. When my school friends visited, they would talk about the sweet apple-tasting drink they were offered in my house as if it were a delicacy. To us it was ordinary, something we drank each day, a boring daily routine.

My mother was difficult to please and got annoyed at everybody, often becoming hysterical. Instead of waiting for the storm to pass, I would challenge her and try to convince her that her behavior and demands were unfair and unjust. She would become even more enraged, and the shouting match would end up with her hitting me with whatever happened to be in her hand. I resented this punishment and considered it unreasonable, excessive, and undeserved. We were not friends. She made a poor role model.

During summer vacation I sometimes hid for hours in some shed, with a pocket full of apples and a book to read, usually a romance novel or a detective story. As she would look for me and send others to look for me, I would go into deeper hiding to avoid chores. In hindsight, I realize she may have been right. Perhaps doing chores was more valuable and a better education than the romance novels, which only provided a rose-colored, idealistic view of life, invariably with a happy ending.

Every night she made me select clothes that I would wear to school the next day and inspected my schoolbag to see whether it was ready. We had different subjects on different days, so the contents of the schoolbag had to reflect each day's schedule. It also had to contain gym clothes on days we had gym. If her inspection revealed flaws, she would wake me and pulled me out of bed to make sure everything was ready for the next morning.

At seventeen I fell in love with Zach. My parents, I later learned, did not approve. Zach was eighteen and in his senior year of high school. I had another year ahead of me. That summer we were inseparable. We swam in the freezing river, and in the fall we rode our bicycles out of town, roaming through the forests looking for cyclamen. How delicate were the flowers hidden in the mossy ground! As delicate as our kisses, our sudden closeness.

"A bunch of flowers for my girl, my love," he said one day, shyly extending a bunch of cyclamen to me.

I took the delicate pink flowers, petals of our love, and we kissed just as gracefully. As we walked through the forest, the sun was not warm, but the fading light played with the breeze in the leaves, creating an intriguing pattern of light and sound, a symphonic wholeness with nature. We kissed again and again, holding each other just a bit tighter each time, and then walked on through the forest until the next hug, the next kiss. At sunset, we rode our bicycles back to town.

On Sunday afternoons during the school year, I told my parents I was spending the afternoon with the chess club but actually I was with Zach. Sometimes we danced in the youth club, clinging to each other; sometimes we walked in the park or the cemetery—our town's favorite date location.

During winter a handball court was transformed into an

ice skating rink, which became the favorite meeting place for everybody regardless of whether they could skate or not. Music blared from two huge speakers all day and late into the evening. There was no place to sit, but that never discouraged people from standing around and coaching their children or just shouting greetings to friends on ice. Zach and I held hands and skated together in rhythm to the music, round and round the rink, almost every day for hours. Some boys skated fast and bumped into others, often on purpose. There was some supervision by the high school physical-education teachers, but it was superficial and lenient. Zach was an excellent skater, because he also played hockey. But with me he skated carefully and slowly, especially on turns, correcting my balance, holding me closer to prevent me from falling, even when I was absolutely in no danger of falling. He would let go of my hand, put his arm around me, stop, pull me closer, and smile mischievously.

"Thought you were going to fall," he would say.

And I would return the smile. "I cannot fall when you are holding me. So hold me closer!"

My parents did not always believe my excuses for coming home late. My father often went looking for me in the town.

During this time after World War II, during the five-year plans to better the economy, few people owned cars. My father, as a physician, had a motorbike, and he took me with him in the fall, just before school started, to vaccinate the children in the surrounding villages. I loved those motorbike trips and felt proud to be helping in this effort to combat infection. He had me spread out his instruments on the white ironed tablecloth invariably provided by the villagers. I handed him the alcohol, gauze pads, and the vaccine vials while the village children lined up waiting to be vaccinated. Although my father's needles looked ominous, hardly anyone ever cried, because he would tell them that he knew this particular village had the bravest kids who would not dare be scared of a vaccination needle—a deceit that worked each time, in each village, with all kids. They all believed they were the bravest.

As the end of the school year approached, we knew Zach would be leaving to go to the university in another town. Our town did not have a university at that time. The imminent separation made us want to melt into each other each time we were together, and we tried to see each other as much as possible. My grades suffered. My favorite subjects were math and physics, but recently I had been drawn toward philosophy, writing, poetry, and literature. I was daydreaming more and studying less. Homework did not get done. Literature was easy to bluff during oral exams, but math could not be bluffed. Zach's grades did not suffer, but he was fretting about his valedictorian speech (which I eventually wrote for him).

It was in March, an unusually warm day, when I lost my virginity. Zach said he had never felt so happy, so alive, and that I made him the happiest man on earth. I was deliriously happy myself, enormously proud of being a woman at seventeen who had made this fantastic man the happiest man on earth. Zach and I did not exactly rush into sex. Young and inexperienced, we stopped many times at different points along the way, until one day it just sort of happened. The tenderness turned into a need, an overwhelming need to continue, and was finally deeply satisfying. We crossed the line happily without regrets, stepping into adulthood. On the way there, I cherished each time Zach told me that he loved me, how beautiful I was. We kissed in a way we had dreamed of kissing. We touched each other hesitantly at first. As we recognized the feeling of pleasure that the touch of each other's bare skin generated, we took great delight in this discovery. Each kiss, each touch, begged another, creating a reason for being alive.

My parents did not approve of our relationship. They said we were too young to marry. They asked Zach not to see me and even asked his father, who had no idea that we were a couple, to talk some sense into his son. His father got angry; probably more from having been left out of the picture and not knowing his son was dating the town physician's daughter. He agreed with my parents that we were too young to marry, and that summer he sent Zach to visit relatives on the Adriatic Sea.

Later that same summer I learned that my family was going to the States. Our immigrant visas had finally been granted. We left our small town, and I never had a chance to say good-bye to Zach. Never had a chance to fully appreciate my womanhood, the passage away from childhood, or to share these feelings with Zach.

In August we boarded a ship and left for the "new world." My father appeared resigned to the need to start a new life at fifty-eight, while my mother was probably dreaming of new clothes, a refrigerator, a vacuum cleaner, a car, a house, and higher social status. As the ship left the port, it started raining. I stood on the deck in the rain. My wet hair clung to my skull as the rivulets of rain mixed with my tears. I looked at the receding beaches and into the clouds, farther and farther, but my hometown was too far to be seen and the distance grew larger. The rain fell harder and harder, my tears turned into sobs and the ship into a vessel of despair.

I always knew I was smart. My grades were good, although I was not very studious and seldom worked hard. And though I excelled in math and physics, and even got a coveted highest grade, equivalent to an A+, in physics on my sixteenth birthday, I yearned to be a journalist. I wanted to travel widely and write about distant lands, distant people, distant events—distant wars, distant struggles for freedom, distant anything—to bring it live to my town.

I started school at six years of age after registering myself. The summer was ending and mornings were much colder. I remember a storm and that the streets were flooded with water that reached up to my knees. A group of us waded gleefully through the muddy waters, a sandal in each hand. I was not allowed on the street by myself. Breaking the rules, as much as splashing around barefoot, gave me an immense sensation of freedom. My mother kept running after me with sweaters or telling me not to go around barefoot anymore. The afternoons were shorter. My friend Natalie had to be home earlier than before, and it seemed our playing house was rushed, with less detail. We even stopped fighting about who was to play the Mother in order to have enough time for the game.

Then one afternoon Natalie announced that she could not come to play with me the following afternoon, because she had to register for school. I asked her what one did in school and whether she thought I could go too.

"Everybody goes to school," she said. "Of course, you can go to school. But you must register first."

"How do you register?" I asked.

"Oh, you tell them your name and where you live and which grade you finished."

"I can give my name and tell them where I live, but I never went to school before. No, no, I can't go to school!" I cried. "They won't know where to put me, if I didn't go before."

"Stupid, of course, they'll know. They'll put you in the first grade," Natalie said with full confidence.

We decided I was to come along to register for school with her the next day. We parted, overjoyed by the secret we shared.

The next day I asked my mother to comb my hair carefully. I also wanted a pink bow in it. She smiled and complied, no doubt surprised and happy that I wanted to look prettier. I ran out of the house way ahead of time and waited in the yard, all ready to go to school and register. When Natalie came, we almost tiptoed to the end of the block, quickly turning the corner and onto another street. I was in mortal fear that my mother would notice my absence and stop me from going to school at the last moment.

I think we ran the rest of the way and, upon reaching the school building, rushed up the stairs. The building was old, dark, and very cold. The stone stairs were indented in the middle, probably from the thousands of feet that went up and down in regular rows of two. Through an open door on the top of the stairs I could see a nun sitting at a desk looking at some papers. Natalie and I, a step behind her, approached the desk. The nun adjusted her glasses. She placed the sheets of paper into two neat piles and looked up.

"Your name, child?" she asked sternly.

"Natalie Horvat," Natalie whispered.

"Speak up, child. Natalie who?"

"Natalie Hor-vat," Natalie said a bit louder, enunciating each syllable of her last name.

"Father's name?"

"Ivan."

"Where do you live?"

So far so good, I thought. I didn't like the nun, but at least I could answer all the questions that would get me to school. Except that I wasn't so sure anymore that coming here had been such a good idea. I felt a word shouted would just tumble down those cold stone steps and fall broken at the bottom. I thought of going home and surreptitiously moved away from Natalie.

But the nun at the desk suddenly smiled and asked, "And what is your name, my child?" The kindness in her voice surprised me, and I answered loudly, suddenly proud of my name. When she found out that I was registering for the first time, she smiled again.

"And your parents. Why didn't they come with you?"

"They are both very busy."

"Well, my dear, just be sure to tell them to bring us your birth certificate tomorrow, will you?"

"Yes, of course, I will. I will."

Natalie raced me down the stone steps and back home. When we got there I realized with consternation that my pink bow was gone. *But mother would forgive me for losing the bow*, I thought, *when she heard about my going to school.*

The nun must have recognized my last name, because she telephoned my father to remind him that a birth certificate was necessary for school registration in the first grade. Later that evening my father sat me on his lap and asked about my adventure with Natalie earlier that day. He asked if I really wanted to go to school, because the customary age for entering school at that time was seven. I had just turned six that spring. I answered seriously, "Yes. I do want to go to school." I kept repeating emphatically, "Yes, I do. I do. I do."

I explained that according to Natalie, school was fun. You learned to write, which I could not yet do; you learned to read, which I already could, more or less; and you sang and played games with other children during recess. And you brought salami sandwiches and an apple that you ate during recess. I loved singing. I loved salami sandwiches. I was eager to become more proficient in reading. Reading was fun. Laughing at my explanations, my father consented and I started the first grade a year early.

Sundays were special when I was growing up. During the week my father was too busy to sit down and talk. Occasionally when he came home from the clinic for the midday meal, he would pull a surprise from a pocket, a piece of chocolate in a shiny wrapper or a thin paperback book. My mom, my sister, and I would linger over food, but father ate fast. After his regular work at the clinic, he attended patients in his private office at home, where his office hours were more flexible. He was always in a hurry to go to his office and take care of his patients.

People waited for him for hours. The village women wore enormous skirts with many petticoats, shawls tied around their chests, and colorful scarves on their heads. Their faces were tired and worn out. To me they all looked alike, ageless. They would cautiously come through the yard and stop just before entering the kitchen, asking deferentially if my father would be able to attend to them soon. Sometimes one of them would pull out a package wrapped in yet another piece of cloth and apologetically hand it to my mother. Sometimes the woman voiced an actual apology, if the package contained only half a dozen eggs. My mother took the packages, set them on the shelf in the kitchen, and asked who the patient was that day. I wondered if she remembered which woman brought eggs and who brought the pint of cream. But I don't think it ever mattered much to my father. He always cared for everyone, as if the egg they left in the kitchen was golden. I suppose he kept some sort of bookkeeping in his head, but the entries and balances were not in amounts of money. We were never poor, but we were never very rich either. It was comforting to know that when people recognized and liked me, it was because they liked and respected my father.

After we had left for the States, one of our former neighbors wrote us that one day a horse carriage stopped in front of our former house. It stood for some time, the horses impatiently huffing, breathing out hot air, a woman reclining in the carriage while a man in an old-fashioned black woolen suit rang the bell. But no one was home and no one answered. Finally our neighbor came out her house and asked the man, a peasant from a village some forty kilometers away, what he was waiting for. He said his wife was sick and he had brought her to the doctor, but apparently the doctor was not home. The neighbor said that the doctor no longer lived there.

"Where does he live now?" he asked.

"The doctor and his family moved to America."

"America?" he asked in disbelief. "Please tell me how to get there. My wife will see no other doctor."

On Sundays my father got up as early as on weekdays, but we had long, leisurely breakfasts with chamber music or the opera playing on the radio and the newspapers spread out over everything. In contrast to the mornings, Sunday afternoons were very quiet. There was hardly anyone on the streets. The townspeople rested after their customary Sunday lunch, listening to the soccer games broadcast over the radio.

On Sundays my father's office was empty. There were no patients in the waiting room. I would approach the office door with caution and knock—just in case. When no one replied, I knocked again, just to be sure. Then I went in, quickly closing the door behind me. The walls were lined with bookcases with sliding glass doors. The anatomy books were my favorite. They had beautiful glossy pictures of all that fascinating machinery inside our bodies. So many nerves. They looked like thin white threads suspended from a white ribbon, not much thicker, traversing our middle longitudinally from the head down. The heart was faintly heart-shaped, but how exactly did it pump? When I was seven or eight, I discovered the intriguing mysteries of anatomy, the pictures showing some distinct differences between boys and girls. These were the pictures I wanted to study in much greater detail.

On one particular Sunday I furtively entered my father's office, took a large anatomy textbook, and carried it into my bedroom, where I hoped I would be undisturbed. I failed to notice that the book was in German.

Engrossed in the fascinating anatomical details, I never saw or heard my father enter the room. Suddenly there was someone looking at the same fascinating details over my shoulder.

"What are you reading, Alexandra?" he asked.

I shut the book quickly. "Oh, nothing. Just looking at some pictures".

"Well, that's about all you can do, since the text is in German."

He laughed. I said nothing.

"Why did you take this book?" he asked.

How could I explain? Feeling guilty for sneaking the book out of his office without asking, I remained silent. He took the book, looked at some pages, saw a smudged fingerprint on the page of female anatomy, and said, "Come to my office. There are other books you might want, ones you can read as well as look at."

"Yes, I'd like that," I agreed. So we walked together to his office and put the German anatomy book back on the shelf.

A few years later, on another Sunday afternoon, the doorbell rang and I went to open the door. Our neighbor, Mr. Cvek, grinned broadly as he greeted me and said, "Tell your father I am here to beat him at chess."

I heard Father laugh. He had heard him.

"Not so quickly, my friend. Today is my turn to win!"

They set up the chess game, and I watched for a while. It got boring because they hardly talked to each other. The chess pieces mysteriously vanished from the board, and a look of annoyance on one man's face would change into a big smile as another piece of the other color followed the first. My father had taught me the basics, but the game was just too slow and boring for me. He was only interested in playing with me when another, more accomplished opponent was not available. Our matches were few and far apart, and I never had enough practice to reach the level where I would present a challenge.

After a while, the doorbell rang again. My father and his friend continued playing, engrossed in their respective strategies. The bell rang again and kept on ringing. I realized it was the doorbell to his office. As I approached it, Father was already there, opening the door wide and letting in an excited crowd of people. Two men carried a young man, his shirt torn and bloody. A knife protruded from his backside. Apparently the young man had been stabbed in front of a movie theater not far from where we lived. Everyone was jostling and pushing and shouting, trying to explain what had happened. My father directed the men carrying the youth to lay him on his office table. After ordering all of them to be quiet, he ushered them out with gentle but obvious authority and closed the door. He called Mr. Cvek to come and help him with the injured youth. I stood in a corner, watching, fascinated. Mr. Cvek eagerly entered the office, looked at the youth, at the shirt, at the knife, at the blood … and fainted.

My father, his hands soapy and dripping, calmly

surveyed the scene and saw me. Supremely efficient, without any trace of excitement or agitation, he said, "Alexandra, come here. I need help."

At ten, I was suddenly infinitely older. Infinitely proud to be treated as an adult.

Some summers I spent with relatives. My mother's relatives were more numerous: my grandmother, my other uncle, his wife, and my two cousins, a boy a couple of years older than I was and a girl a couple of years younger. They owned a farm with cows, pigs, goats, and chickens. There was always something to do and everybody was always busy. Each morning my aunt gave me chores. I actually looked forward to them, which generally meant helping her or one of my cousins with their chores. My cousins tried to get out of them and resented my eagerness, but it was all new to me and I honestly liked being busy. Once I slept in my grandmother's house in a big bed made of dark polished wood with an enormous down comforter. Everything in that bed was oversized, and I sank into down pillows, down everything. But my grandmother was not very talkative. Mostly she murmured things under her breath and was difficult to understand.

I suspected she was getting senile, since she often appeared lost in her memories and did not always recognize me. But everyone treated her with respect, and there was never any mention, much less a frank discussion, of her senility. Much later she came to live with us and soon afterward passed away. While at our house, she floated in and out of her senile world, smiling at some particular event in her memory, calling us by unfamiliar names, not recognizing her surroundings, but perfectly at peace and happy to be where she was.

When not sleeping at my grandmother's house, I stayed in the spare bedroom in my uncle's house. Next to the bed was a large window that stayed open day and night. In front of the window was an apple tree. The apples from that tree were vividly green and red, and when you bit into one, it was pure delight. White and crunchy, sweet and sour, deliciously sour and deliciously crunchy.

As at home, we ate the main meal in the early afternoon. I remember eating yellow wax beans and fingerling potatoes, vegetables I had never seen or tasted before. For supper there was homemade yogurt and thick slices of dark bread, home baked. My aunt was very permissive where I was concerned, and she clearly appreciated my eagerness to join them in whatever task awaited completion. I got up early to collect eggs, some of which were still warm to the touch. I liked the touch of still warm eggs. I helped carry buckets of slops for the pigs, which was poured into troughs, and watched with wonder how eagerly they chomped, nudging each other with their snouts. My cousin taught me how to ride bareback, and his father reprimanded him later. He felt that a city girl should be watched more carefully and not be exposed to the dangers of riding horses that were not used to her. But I had loved it! My cousin, however, never forgave me for talking about it, which was why he wouldn't teach me how to shoot his hunting rifle that summer.

We collected mushrooms and blueberries in the forests on the hills, not far from the house. The mushrooms looked like little yellow-brown fans and grew around tree roots. We had them for lunch the next day, and I learned that there is nothing as delicious as the food you gather yourself. My aunt was a simple cook, but the food she prepared tasted so much better during my summers there. I do not remember whether it was because the physical exertion of farm work made me hungrier, or because of the actual food. The following summer, more distant cousins came to visit as well. That year we often climbed a colossal oak, and high up in its branches we spent hours singing. One of the new cousins, a girl who was a year older than I, knew many songs. With a strong, robust voice, she sang with true enjoyment and taught me to harmonize. We were inseparable.

Other summers I visited my father's brother in a faraway city. His wife, who had been an actress, teased me about my speech and my dialect and good-naturedly corrected my pronunciation. They had no children and seemed happy to have me visit. My paternal uncle was a journalist who traveled a lot and collected stamps. He kept me entertained with stories from his travels and from his and my father's childhood. I learned more about my family background from him than I did from my busy father. In his youth my uncle had been a long-distance runner, and he took me to many track-and-field events. He no longer competed, but frequently refereed at local meets. He was a milder, softer version of my father. Not as tall, not as argumentative, not as hurried, and generally gentler in gestures and behavior. But he smoked smelly unfiltered cigarettes and drank lots of Turkish coffee. He and his wife married when they were in their forties, and they were very tender to each other.

Along with telling stories from his childhood and about his travels, my uncle liked talking about the city and its history, about nature, about how they made cigarettes, about how it was a good thing to run. I argued against that because I hated running long distances. Through his stamp collection he attempted to teach me geography, but somewhat to his disappointment, I was most impressed with those stamps that showed flowers. He knew their Latin names and never tired of telling me what they were, where they grew, how much sun they needed ... I never tired of listening. I felt protected, cared for, loved, enveloped in goodwill whenever I visited him and his wife; and I wished hard that they lived closer to us and that we did not need to travel so far to see them. The days with them passed too quickly, and I was always sorry when my father appeared to take me home. The long journeys back were by rail, and we had to change trains twice. On a few occasions they came to visit us, but it was not the same. Then I had to share them with the rest of the family and did not feel so special.

During the summers immediately after the war, the town organized youth camps on the Adriatic coast. I remember with delight the two summers my parents let me participate by traveling alone and staying at the camp with girls—and boys—my age. The sleeping arrangements were primitive and the genders were, of course, separated. One summer we slept on cots in a large stone building with cold concrete floors. The cots had hay-filled mattresses that were smaller than the cots' wooden frames. The frames had slats that were also not well proportioned, and they slipped when you moved atop the mattress. On more than one occasion there would be a loud crashing noise in the middle of the night as someone, yet again, fell through the slats and woke us.

For breakfast we got two pieces of bread, thickly spread with dark yellow margarine, and a cup of what was called coffee, but was made of some substitute grain and diluted with powdered milk. Lunch was the main meal of the day and it always included soup; a dark multigrain bun—not for health reasons, but because white flour and white bread were much more expensive—a piece of meat, mostly overcooked beef that had produced the soup; lots of beans and potatoes in a great variety of disguises; and a mixed salad. Two or three times a week we had shredded cabbage and carrots, or sometimes lettuce with a lot of canned beets. The most frequent dessert was an apple. When we got a pear, a peach, or grapes, it was a time to celebrate.

But days in the sun and swimming made us hungry, and although we often complained about the boring diet, the plates were never returned with food, and many asked for seconds of beans or potatoes or bread. Supper was a revisited breakfast, but the margarine on the bread was covered by fruit preserves, and instead of coffee we got a watery tea and another piece of fruit.

Although we were on the coast, we seldom ate fish of any kind. Later, when I visited the coast with my parents, I remember eating a lot of fresh tuna. The fish was caught at night by the fishermen and sold in the morning to restaurants and the general public in open markets. Its flavor stayed with me all my life as part of the summers on the Adriatic coast.

Each evening we built log fires and sat around singing, mostly patriotic songs remembered from the war, but there were a few with catchy melodies. One evening somebody complained that the songs were monotonous and loud, and requested that we sing a love song or two, gently, pianissimo. The melodies shyly evolved in the dusk, in the air fragrant with sea breezes, and we sang one song after the other, the ones known from childhood, in intricate and natural harmony, a feeling of nostalgia descending over us—until someone again shouted, "Enough! Enough of these sentimental tunes!" and started another marching howl.

The climate on the coast was hotter than we were used to even in the summer. Swimming in the sea was delightful, wonderfully refreshing, despite the salt. My hair was short, but some of my friends had very long hair that they wore braided. It took a long time to get it dry and comb it out after the salty water tangled it into a sodden, sticky mess. I had the bright idea of offering to cut the long hair of whoever was willing and spent an entire day doing it ... until I cut into an ear. It bled profusely, and the girl was immediately dispatched to the nurse. The nurse came out, shouting at me, threatening to call my parents. I had to promise not to continue with the haircuts. The wounded ear was not, actually, the only reason I stopped cutting hair. One of my closest friends did not like her haircut and wore a kerchief over her head to hide her unevenly layered short hair. It almost became a fashion, and when we returned home and descended the train to greet our parents, they looked bemused until the kerchiefs were off and they realized that almost all of us now sported unevenly cut bobs.

The summers I spent close to home, I was practically attached to a bicycle. All of the children who spent their summer vacations in town went to the river. It was a dangerous river with strong currents, so the town built a skeleton pool out of tree trunks that was suspended in the water, safe for children to swim. Older boys would walk miles up the river. They would jump into its icy waves and be carried downriver in a matter of seconds. At first I did not dare to enter the river and swam in the pool, but as I grew older, I did it a few times. We all knew what to do if caught in rip current, but talking about it was never the same as actually experiencing it. On my first try, I was astonished at how strong the river current was, but doing something dangerous and forbidden was exhilarating. However, I lacked the courage to do it regularly. Mostly we sunned ourselves and played interminable card games, and only went into the water when it was very hot. During the days we played cards at the riverbank, bicycled home for the main meal of the day, and then met up again in the main square, in front of the town hall, in the evening. During summers it was a custom to walk back and forth on the main square in the late afternoon and evening. Almost everybody in town was there, not just the young. We called it korzo.

Not all of us had bicycles. I did not have my own but rode my mother's. If she needed the bike, I would walk to the river beyond the soccer field, through fields of corn and wheat, and then through the forest. If I was alone on the way there, I hurried, especially through the forest, but on the way back I was always with friends, often wearing wet swimsuits underneath hastily thrown-on shorts and shirts, always barefoot jauntily swinging a sandal in each hand.

Since I was a year younger than most of the girls in my class, I sometimes fretted over my sexual development. They all started menstruating before me, sprouted underarm hair, and proudly stuck out their chests to show off their breasts. I had none. I was completely flat chested. Worse yet, I was taller than most. There was one girl in my class who was taller than I was, a year older, and sexually well developed at fifteen. But she was not the tallest girl in town.

The tallest girl, a few years older than I, lived on the street that led to the main square. Her family owned a bakery. She occasionally helped in the store, but did not talk much, and was always well groomed with permed blonde hair. Since she had no brothers or sisters, we believed she was spoiled. I was not particularly friendly with her, but I nevertheless looked for her every day before starting the korzo walk. I certainly did not want to be there alone, the tallest girl, if she was not there already. Next tallest was acceptable.

When it got darker, the girls who had walked with other girls and the boys who had walked with other boys, and who had shouted at and teased the girls who had pretended not to hear, paired off into couples on the way home. This was also a custom, lacking definite dating rules. The couples looked for some privacy in the parks or the cemetery on their circuitous way home. Our cemetery boasted creative landscaping, a synthesis of horticulture and art. Many mausoleums had been built by well-known sculptors, with attached chapels that were part of our cultural history. The bushes and trees were sculpted to form opulent green arcades hiding the silent graves. Those walks home could take an hour or longer, if the couple was really adventurous.

The cemetery and the park surrounding the old castle were almost on my way home. As we began dating, Zach and I took this detour frequently. And just as frequently, we would sneak into an adjoining street or into the park, where we would hide behind a convenient bush when we heard a bicycle approaching. My father's bike had a light fixture attached to a dynamo, which provided electricity for the light. The contraption was rather noisy, and although you could not see the person on the bike clearly in the dark, the hissing dynamo was recognizable. I am not sure whether my father was ready for a confrontation with me and my boyfriend, or whether he just wished to provoke some guilt in his dutiful daughter with his presence. In any case, upon hearing the familiar hissing sound, I would hastily kiss Zach good night and run home to get there before my father.

I have a vivid memory of a time in high school when, during a break between classes, I was distributing the school paper. The paper, which was edited and actually produced— mimeographed—by two boys and me, was free. Still, that day I bragged loudly about its contents and its potential relevance in order to get it distributed and, hopefully, read. I was pleased with the outcome of my sales pitch, because everybody seemed to be asking for a copy. *Selling stuff was not such a difficult job after all*, I thought. My satisfaction was followed by a feeling of dismay and consternation that I was capable of deception, and that this trickery and a certain amount of dishonesty had, indeed, served a purpose. Almost everybody had a copy of the paper and most read it.

The three of us who produced the paper were also members of the high school writing club. It was a forum for young writers, an opportunity to read your work and get peer critique as well as feedback from the teacher in charge. The teacher was uncommonly tolerant and supportive, even of the trite and boring pieces. The writing club met regularly, and although I never missed a meeting, I never submitted anything or read anything that I wrote. After each club meeting, my two friends and I took walks through the parks and talked at length about our plans for the future, typical adolescent stuff. Both boys had often read their work. They teased me about my frequent critiques of others' work while never submitting any short stories or poems of my own. They called me a coward, doubting I could write at all. Though active in other extracurricular activities—track-and-field and choral singing—my writing was of gigantic importance to me and my biggest secret. I had kept a diary since the age of ten, and it included some poems and paragraphs about what I called my "musings" on life. And I was working on a short story.

A conversation I had overhead between my father and another man served as the inspiration for the story. As team doctor, my father had come along to one of my track-and-field meets in a neighboring city. We were traveling by bus. A man got on at the very last moment and as the bus started to move he was thrown off balance. He recognized my father and spoke to him.

"Doctor, it was not my fault."

My father looked at him astonished, not comprehending. "What? What are you talking about? You did not hurt me. It's all right."

The man apologized again. "Doctor, it was not my fault. I did not expect my son to be there. We did not allow children near the construction site. It was not my fault."

"What construction site? What are you talking about? Who are you?"

The man introduced himself and explained that he now lived in another city, separated from his wife.

My father nodded as if he finally understood and mumbled, "Of course, of course. It was not your fault."

The man got off at the next stop, waving good-bye to my father and smiling sadly, seeming unsure about something.

A few days later my father remembered who the apologizing man on the bus was. Several years earlier my father had been called to a construction site after a fatal accident. A child had been hit by falling debris, bricks or some other construction material, and was killed. When they called my father, it was already too late. The only thing he could do was pronounce the child dead. Perhaps out of his own frustration and sorrow, he had admonished the father for letting his son play at the construction site.

The strange interchange on the bus kept coming back to me. I understood my father's anguish for being too late to save the child. On the other hand, I could imagine the child's father's need to assuage the guilt he must have felt at the time of the accident, a guilt that had obviously resided within him for years. I thought about his compulsive need to apologize so many years later to my father during a chance meeting on a bus.

The incident stayed with me, lived within me. I kept thinking of the other father's guilt and my father's complicity, the intricate dynamics of suffering, of the need to dull guilt's edge. I wrote a short story about the incident and kept revising it.

My ambivalence and a healthy dose of insecurity kept

me from showing the draft to anyone before I was sure I had done the best possible job of writing. Just before the next to the last meeting of the writing club, I was told I either had to read something at that meeting or my name would not be included in the club's membership roster. Reluctant, anxious, and very nervous, I agreed to read my short story.

My friends teased me even more when they heard I was going to read, joking about how I'd waited for the last moment to have the last word, to increase everyone's expectation so they'd wait impatiently for this monumental event. But my reluctance to read had nothing to do with any manipulative motives. The only motive was to produce, to write something good—something I could be proud of and that they would not, could not, severely criticize.

My turn came. The silence in the room was challenging, heavy with expectations. I started reading my short story in a low, uncertain voice. As I got caught up in the narrative, I read with more confidence. When I finished, there was an even deeper, longer – louder, silence. I was suddenly too terrified to look up from the page. This silence had a different timbre. Expectant, hoping ... I ached for approval, validation, love. And, boy, did I get it! The others applauded, and I could feel without a doubt that their praise was sincere. The teacher in charge of the club was the first with congratulations. Not one comment was negative. My two friends, my fellow school-paper editors, were at first speechless and then finally conceded that it was a decent piece of writing. I sailed home on my pride, in the company of my two friends, too happy to digest much of what they were saying.

At the end of the school year the writing club had a

literary evening in the town's library. My short story was one of the selected readings, a great honor. This time I read with confidence, and my story was well received. The town's weekly newspaper ran a review of the literary evening, and my story was singled out as the best prose of the evening. The story was also published in the school's paper without any of the usual editorial arguments between the three of us about the value of this particular piece of prose. The agreement was unanimous, and all three of us were equally pleased with that issue of the paper, because it included this particular story.

At that time there were no copy machines. Producing a high school paper involved a lot of overtime and long hours with the mimeograph machine, which copied each page into a wet product with many smudges and stains, hardly readable at times. Many a page had to be discarded, but eventually the acceptable pages were collated into a readable issue and with some one hundred copies, each smudged page, each stain, a matter of pride and a proof of our collaborative hard work.

OUR FIRST FEW WEEKS in the United States, we stayed with distant relatives of my mother in Levittown, a town on Long Island that became infamous for its unique urban design. Not only the houses, but the porches, garages, and the lawns were identical. People joked that a drunk would have a hard time finding his own home. There were no sidewalks that I remember, and one needed a car for every single errand. I was not used to weekly grocery shopping and wondered why one needed a car to buy milk or stamps. This was the era when people still wrote letters and postcards, although I was baffled why one would write a card and then stuff it into an envelope. We often sent postcards from vacations, but the custom of sending birthday cards, Christmas cards, and especially Valentine cards was unfamiliar and strange.

Our birthday presents were mostly books, and we did not need a card to identify the giver. The gifts did not get mixed up; there were not that many. Besides, I wondered why one needed an envelope for a card with a brief message that would fit on a postcard, and mailing it would cost less.

I was told by my mother's relatives that it was not polite to give postcards with birthday gifts or send them for Christmas. The privacy of the message had to be protected, I guess ... and the post office made more money.

While we stayed in Levittown, we made trips to Long Island beaches. In contrast to the Adriatic Sea with one of the most scenic coasts in Europe, Long Island beaches stretched for miles and were covered with soft, clean, beautiful sand—not a pebble or rocky, algae-coated crevice in sight. Their immensity was startling. But then, one expected that everything big would be in the USA. I loved walking at the edge of the ocean, water caressing my feet, thinking that Long Island beaches were magnificent. But the journey to the beaches took several hours, and we saw no people. On the highways there were only cars, and as I looked out of the car window at the houses we passed, they all seemed closed and deserted. Not a person anywhere, no children playing in the yards, no animals, just cars. I felt transported to a different world, way out in the future, mechanistic and uninhabited by humanity.

My mother's relatives were working people; Edmond worked in construction and Mary in an office. Each workday they left early in the morning, before we were up. During our first days, Mary explained, very seriously, the American customs surrounding meals. One was supposed to have juice, coffee, and two pieces of "toast" for breakfast; a sandwich and a glass of milk for lunch; and dinner was the main meal of the day. For dinner one had two cooked vegetables, one of them being rice, potatoes, or "pasta," and a piece of meat. A mixed salad of fresh vegetables was eaten first. On Thursdays and Sundays there was cake for dessert. On other days there was no dessert. We could have "snacks."

Prior to coming to the States I had a few English lessons from a young woman who had spent a few summers in England to improve her English. She was fair-skinned and wore only pastel colors, giving an impression of insipid and anemic expertise. She gave private lessons to those who could afford them. She didn't have many students, because English was not very popular. I hated her and her priggishness. She made me wash my hands before each lesson, and notes had to be started on a fresh page with a newly sharpened pencil. I had to use a pencil so that offending items could be corrected immediately by erasing them. But she did tell me about toast, and I eagerly awaited my first breakfast in the United States, when I would be introduced to this delicacy of toasted bread.

I was a little suspicious of warmed bread. Freshly baked bread was often still warm and had a most delicious crust. We sometimes warmed up stale bread in the oven to improve it before serving. So of course, I had misgivings about eating bread that was perfectly square in shape and bought in a plastic wrapper. Even worse, it was already sliced. But when I spread salted butter on a slice of toast, it was heaven. I would have eaten the whole loaf if allowed, and a measly two slices were an outrage. But my family and I were guests and there was no way I could complain. Needless to say, all of my lunch sandwiches were on toast.

As a child I loved salami sandwiches, and my mother's relatives provided us with a variety of cold cuts for lunch, along with something they called mayonnaise. My mother made mayonnaise on special occasions at home and usually served it with cooked vegetables in a dish called Russian salad. Here, the mayonnaise came in a jar. I would spread it on a piece of toast and add a slice of ham or salami, tomato or a pickle, and cover it with another slice of toast also smeared with mayonnaise. Delicious! I was a great fan of American cuisine from the start.

Soon I discovered another delicacy: the grilled cheese sandwich. I could have eaten lunch all day long, not missing what they called dinner at all. Dinner was a quick affair, prepared in minutes. The vegetables were often already cooked and emptied from a can into a pot to be warmed. Nothing was added. I found them particularly tasteless, but my mother's relatives told us that they were full of vitamins. Most meat was broiled, but occasionally a chicken was roasted. The mixed salad was mostly lettuce with quartered tomatoes and slices of unpeeled cucumber or green peppers, and we ate it with a creamy white or a pink "dressing," another new food. Neither of them looked or tasted appealing. Our salads at home had had lots of onion and garlic and were prepared with salt, pepper, vinegar, and oil, not buried alive under a gooey "dressing". Even when one ordered a mixed salad in a restaurant, different vegetables were plated in their own individual islands.

The most mysterious part of the meal customs was the one about dessert on Thursdays and Sundays. The Sunday dessert was less of a mystery. At home we often had guests for Sunday dinners (eaten at midday), and my mother, who was a good cook when she felt like cooking, made a variety of desserts, seldom repeating them from Sunday to Sunday. Her cakes and puddings were too good to produce leftovers. In Levittown, a fresh nut cake was baked each Sunday, each of us got a single piece, and the rest was wrapped in a moist white cloth and saved for Thursday. The nut cake was delicious and each slice begged another, but no way was the second piece offered or served until the next Thursday. In my mind the nut cake probably improved in taste with memory, because I remember craving the second piece with all my heart.

In my own home, I have never served any dinners with individual portions on the plates, including desserts. I have always served the food in serving bowls, for everybody to serve themselves as much or as little as they liked. We were not hungry in Levittown, but so many food rules and the restriction of choice were hard to take.

During my childhood, in the days after World War II, the variety of food was limited. We ate more or less the same thing every day for what seemed like years, but I did not remember any rules about not eating more than a slice of nut cake or two slices of bread. In America, the country that boasted unlimited freedom of choice, the rules of behavior were burdensome and left a deep impression on me.

In order to learn English, it was suggested to us by the more experienced, less recent immigrants, that we watch television, read *Reader's Digest*, and go to the movies. *What about classes conducted by trained teachers?* I wondered. *Any books?* I was told that classes were fine, but I would only learn spelling and grammar in classes, I would not learn how to speak and communicate with ordinary people, the shopkeepers, supermarket clerks, ticket sellers ... The books were not helpful for simple everyday conversations. So it seemed logical, once we had our own apartment that among the first things we bought once we had mattresses, a table, and chairs, was a television set. Watching television became a daily activity.

It took time to get used to the nine-to-five workday and a main meal in the evenings, but it was easy to be persuaded to watch television. We watched police and hospital dramas and sitcoms. Such programs definitely enriched our spoken vocabulary, especially with the latest slang expressions. Talk shows were difficult at first, and stand-up comedy was incomprehensible. Often, not getting the gist of a joke, we wondered why everybody else was laughing. Humor is difficult for foreigners when their language skills are evolving.

This is the reason, I think, why foreigners are often considered humorless and slow witted, when they do not get jokes that any American idiot laughs at with obvious delight. I remember how a postal clerk reacted to my rudimentary Spanish when I was buying stamps when I was much older and Carlos and I lived in Caracas. I asked for stamps to mail letters to the United States and to Europe, and to send postcards. The stamps were of different denominations. After a brief negotiation in my broken Spanish, I asked for ten of each to simplify matters. I mentally calculated the total in bolivars, the Venezuelan currency, while the clerk wrote down the details of the purchase, and added up the total on a piece of paper.

"*¿Son 120 bolivares, no es cierto?*" I asked.

He looked up at me, genuinely surprised and, perhaps, a bit annoyed, "*¿Señora,*" he said, "*como es que usted sabe sumar, pero no puede hablar?*"

The postal clerk wanted to know how come I could add but could not properly express myself in Spanish.

Most Americans did not have much experience with foreigners at that time and reacted similarly to anyone who could not speak clearly, considering them dim-witted and unintelligent. People they met who had poor language skills were often uneducated, mentally challenged, slow... Of course they could not add. Of course they had no math skills. Of course they were too stupid to get the jokes!

Watching television was entertaining, but in the beginning it was also frustrating because of the commercials. Their intrusion into the program was totally unwelcome. Why was this person suddenly talking about toilet paper in the middle of a police drama? It would take us a moment to realize that the segment did not belong within the narrative. Why the constant interruptions? Why couldn't all the ads be aired at the end of the program? We had no idea how the television programs were produced, and that the stirring dramas and hilarious sitcoms had to be financed in some way. It took us years to get used to the commercials and even find them useful. Nevertheless we were influenced by them and bought products in the supermarkets that we remembered from the ads. At least the baffling choices in cleaning products became less confusing.

On the other hand, shopping for food in the States was so easy! Everything was labeled, measured, packaged. You did not have to bargain. Prices did vary from supermarket to supermarket. The reason and logic for that escaped us at first, but we soon learned to shop at the place with the lowest prices. We willingly and enthusiastically adjusted to capitalism and the idea of the free market. In my letters to my friends in Yugoslavia, I described these practices in details, complaining that in America you had to waste time to "shop around" for the best price of everything. You could not just go to a shoe store and buy the same pair of shoes as everybody else for the same price. Another shoe store had the same exact pair, but for a different price. Not only that, but there were hundreds—yes, hundreds—of different shoe styles for the same price. There were such wonderful options in buying shoes. There were options in buying toothpaste. There were options in buying food. I could, due to options, create a unique person and not be my usual old self. The life of an immigrant was full of astonishing surprises, full of choices, so unexpectedly rich.

Although discouraged by my mother's relatives from taking classes or reading books, I got a library card as soon as I located the nearest library in our new neighborhood. The first books I borrowed were mysteries by Agatha Christie. The often stilted dialogue was not particularly helpful, but I learned new words at a breakneck speed. The intriguing plot urged me to read on, even when I did not understand each word, in order to identify the murderer. As I read, the same word would be repeated in different contexts, and I would guess its meaning without recourse to a dictionary. In this way I learned many new words by context. I hated the dictionaries at first, because each unknown word was explained by a set of new unknown words. It was so time consuming to get the right meanings from the multiple entries. So I am indebted to Agatha Christie, because as her books kept me reading to find out what happened at the end, my vocabulary grew, making the business of looking up words less cumbersome. Eventually I graduated from Agatha Christie to American detective stories and the rest of American fiction. That first year in the United States,

I read Steinbeck, Fitzgerald, and Hemingway. Again. But this time in the original.

When I realized I could also read plays, my weekly trips from the library included Tennessee Williams, Eugene O'Neill, and Henrik Ibsen, my favorite playwrights. Shakespeare was much too difficult, even with a dictionary—even on the stage!

From Levittown we moved closer to the city. I was the first one to get a job as a filing clerk in an insurance company situated on the thirtieth floor of a building in mid-Manhattan. My job was to take little pieces of paper that were spit out by a teletype machine and file them alphabetically by the last name of the insured client into large folders. Those large folders were piled onto a cart, which was taken to another floor and, I assume, filed alphabetically according to the last names again. The work was mindless and did not require much knowledge of the language, which was good, since my English at the time was poor. But after a while I could recite the English alphabet very fast, without errors or hesitation.

After work on Mondays I took the subway to a brownstone on the Upper East Side where some rich college-educated ladies gave free classes in English to immigrant professionals, mostly from Europe. Most of my classmates were young doctors who had come to the States to further their education and be trained in different medical specialties. We learned little grammar, and to my delight no one was interested in testing my knowledge, or lack of it, of irregular verbs. My father had made us practice those on the boat crossing during our journey to the States. The ladies were beautifully dressed in beige or navy wool sweaters and wore pearls and colorful silk scarves with the word Hermes or Chanel spelled on the edges. Their nails were manicured, and during hot days of spring—and even throughout the summer, I imagined—they wore stockings and gloves. Of course, that was ridiculous, but I felt obliged to imitate them to assure success in America. The classes were useful, concentrating on everyday conversation. We all were given a chance to practice talking, engaging each other with simple yet intelligent conversation. The homework was almost nonexistent. The doctors would not have time to do it anyway.

At work I must have been a rarity, because other girls loved explaining things and educating me in the ways of America. We had lunch at Schrafft's or at Chock full o'Nuts, restaurants without waiters. At Schrafft's, the sandwiches were displayed on little shelves with glass fronts, and a shopper could make a selection by sight. The girls ordered for me in the beginning. Later, when alone, I would order the same lunch to be on the safe side, and not be surprised by what was set in front of me as a result of a misunderstanding or a mispronounced word. Reading the menu was not enough, because many items were still unfamiliar. It took a long time before I felt brave enough to order something different, such as raisin bread with cream cheese. It sounded exotic, but when I had the courage to try it, it was surprisingly edible. Still, I seldom ventured into new restaurants by myself to prevent any embarrassment of not recognizing dishes on the menu or not ordering anything that I could not pronounce.

My coworkers constantly bombarded me with questions about the life I had left. Wasn't it oppressive living in a Communist country? they would ask. Not Communist but socialist, I would patiently correct.

"Socialist, Communist, what's the difference?" they would ask, utterly uninterested in finding out.

"Living there was fine."

"Did you date?"

"What do you mean, 'date'?"

"You know, go out with boys?"

"Of course!"

"Did you have a boyfriend?"

"Yes, I had a boyfriend."

"Did you go dancing?"

"Yes, we went dancing, sometimes."

"What car did he drive?"

"He did not have a car."

"Then how did you get around?"

"Mostly we walked."

This was not the right answer. It generated pity for me for growing up in a socialist regime and for all the young people living such simple, boring car-less lives. But when I tried to describe "socialist" dating customs in more detail, the pity grew to such proportions, they felt they needed to hug me and protect me from my sad memories. Their emotional outbursts were completely incomprehensible, but nice. Someone was concerned about my well-being; someone was interested in educating me in the ways of this new culture.

But the dating issue remained shrouded in perplexity. Dating was a totally foreign concept to me. At home we all knew each other and went to dances in groups. If I wanted to dance with my boyfriend, Zach, I did. If I wanted to dance with any other boy, I did. We were all friends. The exclusivity that came as a consequence of dating or "going steady" was totally unfamiliar. All the places of interest in my hometown were within walking distance, so why would we need a car? Any other places that were a bit farther did not present a problem. One could always borrow a bicycle.

Whenever I tried to describe life in a socialist country, my words were dismissed with a shrug.

"Poor Sandy," they'd say. "She doesn't know any better!"

They shortened Alexandra to Sandy despite my many protests, because it sounded more American—tamer—to their ears. Disappointed with their lack of interest in a serious political discussion, I stopped trying to explain socialism, excusing their general ignorance with my lack of language skills.

I would have antagonized them even more had I tried to explain the economic, political, and social differences of the several nations that had adopted Marxism as their fundamental economic and political theory. The governments of the Soviet Union's republics, as well as such countries as Albania, Hungary, Bulgaria, Romania, East Germany, Czechoslovakia, Yugoslavia, China, and Cuba, were all different. Many of these Marxist nations, so-called people's republics, evolved into authoritarian states with stagnant economies. The definition of socialism varied from country to country. Most of them would not call themselves Communist.

With certain unease, not wanting to be perceived as disloyal to my new country, I remembered the Marxist seminars I was expected to attend on Sundays during high school. This was a privilege and honor granted to those of us with good grades. The Marxist analysis began with an analysis of material conditions. The socialist system of government was viewed as inevitable, where control of the means of production would be in the hands of the proletariat, the working masses. According to Marxist theory, capitalism concentrated power and wealth within a small segment of society, which gained wealth through exploitation. This resulted in a stratified society of unequal opportunities. Socialism, on the other hand, was about bringing society up to the level of modern technology. Its primary goal was to achieve social equality and the distribution of wealth based on an individual's contribution to society. The Soviet model dictated a centrally planned economy through five-year plans, directed by a single party, the Communist Party.

The People's Republic of China followed Mao's version of Communism, although the Chinese never accepted the term Maoism. They viewed it as a pejorative. Chile's Salvador Allende was democratically elected and formed a coalition government, in which the Communists were in the minority and the most radical group was the pro-Mao socialists. Yugoslavia abandoned the rigid system of centrally planned economies in 1948, when Tito broke away from the Soviet bloc. The country remained a single-party system for years, but the economic system eventually decentralized into a self-management system, based on the cooperative social relationship, the worker-owned industries, and the profit-sharing policies. Worker's self-management was promoted on all levels of society. Yes, individual choices were curtailed in all Marxist-based systems, but life was very different depending on whether one lived in the Soviet Union, China, Cuba, Yugoslavia, or Chile.

The ignorance of the average American secretary

seemed abysmal. Although I granted my coworkers their right to think me brainwashed by my Marxist upbringing, I reserved a private right to think them ignorant of the world outside the United States. To argue or to try to educate them about socialism did not seem prudent. To be perceived as a covert Communist would have been foolishly dangerous, especially since I wished with all my heart to embrace this new culture and its many benefits.

As soon as I had saved enough money, I enrolled in an evening English class for speakers of foreign languages at the university. Upon paying the fee, I was given an IBM card with my name, level of the English class, time the class met, location of the classroom, and the seat number.

For my first class I arrived early, right after work. Once I located the right building and the right floor, I entered a large classroom with rows of numbered seats. A young woman approximately my age was seated in the middle of the middle row, reading a magazine. As I entered the room, she looked up and closed the magazine. I could see that it was *Vogue*.

As my IBM card had a seat number, I asked her timidly, "Do we have to sit according to the seat numbers on the card?"

"No, not at all." She smiled. "You can sit anywhere you want."

Encouraged by her smile, I decided to press my luck. "In that case, I'll sit next to you."

And I promptly plopped my bag into the seat between us and pulled out a paperback with the intention of reading it for the half hour before class began. But the other woman turned toward me and spoke,

"Since we are sitting next to each other, let me introduce

myself. My name is Yelena. Spelled with a *Y*." She smiled warmly again and extended her hand for a handshake.

The name *Yelena* sounded very familiar. Although not spelled with a *y*.

I shook her hand and, taking a chance, replied in my native tongue. *"A ja se zovem Alexandra."* Unable to control my laughter, I told her my name was Alexandra.

Yelena laughed, too, and continued in the same language. "How on earth did you know?"

"Well, it was not very difficult when you said your name was Jelena. Although I would not think of spelling it with a *y*. There is no *y* in our alphabet."

"No, of course there isn't. But here I want to make sure I'm not called *Je*-lena. You know, like *je*-lly beans."

Yelena was a fashion designer and worked on Seventh Avenue. Her boyfriend, who worked at the reception desk of a hotel, took evening college classes, one of which met on the same evenings as our English class. Soon the three of us became inseparable.

After class we roamed through Greenwich Village, sat for hours in our favorite coffeehouse drinking tea, deep in arguments about fashion, poetry, and plans for the future. Yelena's boyfriend was a poet.

That summer we took long subway rides to the beach on weekends, bags packed with sandwiches and iced tea made by Yelena's mother. We read poetry and plays aloud, taking turns, practicing English, correcting one another. Yelena's boyfriend often read his poems. I still remember one of them because he wrote it for me, teasing me about being tall and about my ambition to become a journalist. The poem was witty, and it asked a reader to imagine

Alexandra still growing while her husband of many years had already stopped.

When Yelena and her boyfriend married, they moved from New York to New England, and sadly, we lost touch.

After a year of working in the insurance company, filing little pieces of paper into folders and being paid for it weekly; and even getting free coffee, chocolate milk, or tea during my two breaks, I decided to go back to school. My savings from a year's worth of work were spent in a second when I paid for the first semester at the university.

Before I was enrolled in the college, I attended an interview that would place me, a foreigner, into the proper level of English. I came to the interview with Hemingway's *For Whom the Bell Tolls*. It was not intentional. I always carried books on the subway to read. This was just the latest item on my subway reading list. The professor interviewing me spied the book.

"Whose book are you hiding there?"

"Mine."

"You are reading Hemingway?"

"Yes, I like him. This is the second book of his I am reading in English."

"Are you using a dictionary to read it?"

"No, he is a very clear writer. Mostly dialogues. Not as difficult—or as boring—as Proust."

"You read Proust?"

"Yes, but in translation. Very long sentences. Pages-long sentences. I much prefer Hemingway."

He asked me what I planned to major in.

"I think I would like to major in journalism," I said.

He placed me in the regular freshman English class, not

the one for foreign speakers of English. At first I viewed this outcome with a certain amount of pride. But it was not to my advantage. Getting a good grade in this class proved a lot of extra work. Had I been placed in the English class for foreigners, an A would have been much easier to get. But I was too inexperienced in those matters to request a transfer.

I majored in journalism and minored in biology. The language did not come easily. Writing is hard in a foreign language. The complexity of thought does not always match the verbal outcome on paper. It is reduced and simplified by the available vocabulary, until it morphs into trite observation, lacking the subtlety of verbal contrast used by an intelligent innate speaker. As vocabulary builds, a person can express nuances of thought more precisely and more honestly. In the beginning, the nonnative speaker has to use the available instruments, cut the thoughts with clumsy hands and big scissors, like a toddler using scissors for the first time. The shapes of the objects are approximate; the shape of thoughts imprecise and fractured. Agility increases with practice. The correspondence between the written word and the thought improves by degrees. Where thoughts were once expressed in black and white or a muted gray palette, colors emerge. Nuances evolve, and the thoughts become recognizable when clothed in their new written attire. All of this takes time and effort. In the meantime, one has to deal with the anguish of being misperceived, misunderstood ... different.

Thrown into this new way of life and this new culture, with its new codes of conduct and ways of thinking, I became curious about the etiology of thoughts, opinions, beliefs, attitudes, and feelings of others. I tried to identify their perceptions, tracing their reasoning and views. I wanted to find out what motivated them—how they were influenced and by what circumstances. I did not want to be critical, just observant, nonjudgmental. I was eager to learn. I felt an urgent need to analyze meticulously the most insignificant details of my daily life; to make comparisons, recognize the similarities, isolate the hurts, and accept the improvements.

My primary motivation was not to simply identify, categorize, label, and store the impressions, but to bridge the gap between me and others and outline our mutual common territory—that safe ground where we could exist as partners and, ultimately, friends. I thought this process of analysis would be a worthwhile topic for my future writing. I hoped to explore the conflict between the emotional and the rational aspects of my everyday existence, which I believed others could identify with. We could then share our experiences and agree about the outcome. I needed to find and describe that mutual common ground, the familiar part of identical experience, so as not to feel like an outsider. In my writing I wanted to communicate precisely who I thought I was; be honest and revealing. It was not just a matter of language. I needed to learn more about myself.

My new environment seemed conducive to this subjective exploration, since everyday encounters resulted in persistent little failures and defeats—and some successes. Although I did not always feel an outsider, there were days when the connection to the rest of humanity was more tenuous and needed reinforcing. At times groping through my inner self in search of the essence of who I was, rummaging among the emotional surfaces and textures, I felt closer to an understanding of my persona. In juxtaposition to the feelings, thoughts, and opinions of others, I was a step closer to solving the puzzle of a hypothetical human persona, representative of all of us.

Was this immersion into a new culture shaping a better person? Was I forced into evaluating my worth as a person just because there was a failure of communication? Was language imposing a constraint on experience, or was the failure of communication making me a more accurate judge of value? Was I becoming a more knowledgeable, more precise observer? Because of the unavoidable hurts and failures, was I forced to reevaluate the most basic principles of being? Would the effort in weathering defeat shape a better person, a more observant observer, a better writer? I wondered whether my writing would have the power to transcend and become a strong current, or be a mere trickle that merges imperceptibly.

Some of us are afraid to expose blemishes and quirks, and shroud the inner self in secrets. I wanted it naked and exposed. I never thought that revealing it would make me more vulnerable. I believed that there was strength and courage in honesty. Those personal aches or accomplishments, however small and amorphous they might appear when viewed from the perspective of the universal human puzzle, I wished them to be contributory. I did not want to write pure fiction, pure imagination. Fiction is entertaining. Art is enjoyable, even when draped in secrets and unattainable. My intention, however, was to reveal, disrobe, uncover. I wanted my writing to be an investigation, a search for truth, a scrutiny of emotional complexity. I wanted to explore those aspects of all of us that make us similar, not unique. I wanted acceptance and approval; a tolerance for the mosaic of our differences.

In my senior year in college I met Carlos. I was lonely and insecure. My family's social status had changed. The societal emphasis was on wealth rather than on education, professional merit, or moral value. It affected all of us, but mostly my father. This late in life, he labored to learn English, and then to relearn medicine. He successfully passed the medical board exams on the first try, and fulfilled all the requirements for the license to practice medicine, but he underestimated the monetary benefit for the services he could offer and was satisfied with a salaried position in a hospital.

My mother was happy with the improvements as far as the household chores were concerned. There was central heating, hot and cold water, a washing machine and a dryer, a refrigerator and a car. However, she misinterpreted the progress in the standard of living as a boost in social status and not what it actually was—a plunge into economic lower middle class. We could easily afford movies, but not eating out in restaurants where the tables were covered with tablecloths. To go to the theater to see a play or to the opera marked a very special occasion. We could afford to go on short trips, but most vacations were spent at home.

Socializing was limited to a small group of people. Since we could not afford for me to live on campus, I commuted to the university, which limited my social interactions. Most of my friends in college were foreign students like me, and we amused ourselves by comparing the ways in which we were unique.

Carlos was older. No longer a student, he seemed well established in his ways. Although he, too, was an immigrant, life in the States did not appear mysterious or difficult to him. On the contrary, to Carlos, it was full of potential gain and possibilities. He had a good job and earned a salary. He could afford things which to me were luxuries.

We dated, had sex, often quickly, surreptitiously, and in strange places. I got pregnant and we married. And then the sex stopped. Carlos claimed that sex made everything "dirty," and he could not have dirty sex with the mother of his child.

He traveled extensively on business throughout South America. I was lonelier than before my marriage. With marriage came an end to the freedom to observe the world and be the sole judge of the meaning of events. Although I had a need to please my husband—I felt that as his wife, I had a responsibility to make him happy—his feelings and reactions seemed unfamiliar, displaced. The age difference between us divided us into separate generations. As the marriage progressed, I began to resent the boundaries that had suddenly appeared in my life.

From the beginning of our marriage I sensed that his mother did not approve of the marriage. His parents did not come to the wedding, did not send a gift, and did not ask to meet me or my parents. Perhaps it was because I was pregnant when we married. To their conservative Catholic minds, this was clearly a sin. Perhaps Carlos's mother thought I had planned the pregnancy to push him into marriage. Actually, I had exerted no pressure, and neither had my parents. Carlos was ready to get married, and to me he seemed secretly overjoyed with the outcome. According to a list he once showed me, I fulfilled most of the criteria he specified for his future wife.

At first I was unhappy with the unplanned pregnancy. Lonely and isolated during those college years, I overestimated the change in dating Carlos. Now I hoped that marriage and motherhood would banish depression and give me reasons to plan a rosier future. Not that I had a complete picture of the future, the married life and motherhood. The picture was sketchy at best, mostly based on what I hoped my new life would not be, rather than on any actual goals and accomplishments.

The only thing I was determined to continue was my studies. I saw no conflict between wanting a professional life and being a good wife and a good mother. It never occurred to me that this might create serious problems.

Carlos was an only child. His hardworking parents, who owned a bar and a bakery in Caracas, had spoiled him. His mother seemed to dominate the family structure and dynamics. Carlos was eager to please her. When he mentioned his father, it was obvious he had affection for him, but there was not much respect.

He professed to love his mother, but the feeling was mixed with fear of potential penalties for not pleasing her. Her letters were filled with criticism, complaints, and demands. She kept reminding Carlos that he was her only son and had certain responsibilities toward her, which were usually clearly spelled out, although not outrageous. Mostly they were requests for money for some sudden unforeseen repairs or fees. As far as I could tell Carlos always complied, regardless of the strain it might put on his own finances.

Although well educated, with an MBA from an Ivy League institution, Carlos was in many respects self-taught and self-made. He worked as a refrigerator repairman to support himself through college and graduate school, and possessed a union card of which he was extraordinarily proud. He loved the opera and poetry. His favorite poets were all dead or were his former classmates from *collegios* in Caracas. His persona harbored many contradictions, in part from his prudish Catholic upbringing, in part from his travels, and in part from years spent living on his own. When we met he was an established businessman. On our first date he took me to the opera and later to a café, where he talked about his extensive travels and told numerous anecdotes. He loved talking and hardly ever listened. In the beginning it was all amusing, especially his anecdotes, but eventually he started repeating them too often and I lost interest.

Carlos liked the "good things" in life. He dressed well and expensively, spending much time in front of the mirror as he changed shirts and ties, talking to himself until he achieved just the right image. Looking at himself put him in a good mood. Talking put him in a good mood. He was a tall and attractive man, neat and well groomed. In his younger days he wore a mustache and bragged that it made him look like Errol Flynn. His gray eyes changed color according to his mood, from a pale blue-gray to a steely dark gray, almost black, when he was annoyed. His sweaters matched his many moods.

Carlos had an extensive family and many friends of all ages. He actively followed South American politics in the sense that he read several newspapers every day and was up to date with everything that was going on in Argentina, Chile, Venezuela, and Brazil. His business trips on behalf of his company were numerous and took him all over South America. He loved traveling and often changed his itineraries without consulting his bosses or me. His secretary would call me to ask when Carlos was scheduled back from the trip. In the beginning I lied or invented numerous excuses for the missed flights, blaming the airlines for overbooked flights or on the weather and nonexistent storms. When he finally got back and I asked why he'd missed his flight, he would switch the conversation skillfully to the presents he'd brought and how he'd missed us, and then he'd start calling people to tell them he was back.

Most of our vacations were extensions of his business trips, visiting his family in Venezuela and Argentina. My first meeting with his mother did not go so well. She begged Carlos to visit her and seemed eager to meet his son's wife and her grandson. It was soon obvious that she had formed an image of us to her liking. We came to Caracas from Buenos Aires, where Carlos had some business to take care of and where we stayed in an expensive hotel. I had long hair at the time and was looking forward to have it shampooed and styled in the hotel's beauty salon. The stylist suggested a henna rinse for my dark brown hair, and feeling adventurous, I agreed. Afterward I kept looking in the mirror, posing and imagining situations in which the luxurious reddish glint in my hair would be admired by those around me and would bring forth deserved compliments.

When we got to Caracas, his mother, all three hundred pounds of her, leaning on a cane, was already out of the house, impatiently waiting at the gate. She greeted her son with a long embrace, kissed and hugged Jason, who had approached her with trepidation. Letting go of Jason and looking at me, she exclaimed with a triumphant smile, "I knew it! I knew it would be a redhead who would steal my son away from me."

It was downhill from then on... No matter what I did, I could not please her.

Her health was poor. She was dangerously overweight and had diabetes, which was complicated with heart disease, and she walked with difficulty. She did not live long after we met. Carlos's father lived with relatives until his death a few years after her.

I made a point of learning Spanish because I loved its melodious yet masculine sound. A phonetic language, Spanish was easy to read and pronounce correctly, except perhaps for the double *r*'s. Spanish is truly a beautiful language, and when I was finally able to read Gabriel Garcia Marquez in the original, I marveled at his wealth of expression and the musicality of some words that in English sounded ordinary.

Carlos's relatives were not at all impressed by the fact that I could speak Spanish. To them it was perfectly normal. They never spoke English when I was present, although most were more fluent in English than I was in Spanish. They were critical of me for not teaching Jason to speak Spanish immediately, as his first language, and for exclusively speaking English with him.

"Why are you speaking English with Jason and not his mother tongue?" Carlos's numerous cousins would ask. "His father's mother tongue is Spanish. You are his wife! Speak Spanish to your son."

"Jason was born in the States," I would counter.

The language was frequently an issue. I almost felt guilty at times—I really liked Spanish—but Jason had been born in the States. His native tongue was English. There was not a doubt in my mind that Jason would eventually love Spanish as I did, but he needed to learn English first.

On one of our trips to Chile, I heard Joan Manuel Serrat speak and sing at a rally in a sports stadium and fell in love with his songs. He was a young medical student at that time fighting for a free Cataluña. It all sounded so romantic. His music was set to Antonio Machado's poetry, and I got as many cassettes as possible.

I still listen to Joan Manuel Serrat and his music and still read Machado, although Carlos is dead now and Serrat's music is on CDs. And Jason speaks Spanish fluently.

Our marriage was doomed from the beginning. I failed to perceive the warning signs, or ignored them, hoping that the situation would improve and get better once Jason was older and I was out of school. Carlos seldom showed any vulnerability or need for succor or comfort. He had little need for sex, never delighting in spontaneous sensuality. Any attempt on my part to include a sensual touch as part of lovemaking was rebuked. There was no foreplay. Sex was a duty. Yes, he wanted to be good at it, but not necessarily so he could give pleasure. Pleasure was a by-product. He was not required to give pleasure. I was his wife.

He often bragged about me being in graduate school, that I was smart enough to have finished college and smart enough to enter graduate school. But journalism and film were not legitimate courses of study, because in his mind they would not lead to professions that yielded salaries worth mentioning. More like hobbies. The only type of profession he seemed to acknowledge was business.

And despite my being smart enough for graduate school, he never gave me an opportunity to discuss any important topics with him. If I broached a serious subject or challenged his point of view about something, he would turn it into a joke, change the subject, or leave the room.

Although we had dinner parties with his friends, there were none with my friends. I did try once. I invited two couples from graduate school. The four of them were all still students, making ends meet on student earnings, with part-time teaching jobs. Both husbands were PhD candidates in neuroscience, studying vision. During dinner Carlos kept bragging about his trips to South America and how much extra money he made on those trips because he was paid a per diem. He dismissed their efforts to talk politics or economics, belittling their knowledge of current events because they were *scientists.* They did not go out into the world, but spent their time looking at computer screens in dark rooms. The meal grew uncomfortable. My friends became quiet, and immediately after dinner Carlos went to the bedroom to read Argentine newspapers, leaving me to entertain my friends alone. At school, they avoided me later, pleading large workloads and no time for coffee.

When we entertained his friends, Carlos was center stage, center of attention. There was no end to his amusing anecdotes from his trips, his jokes, the wine and good times. He also liked to sing and did so often when inebriated, but he could not carry a tune. As his wife, he was proud of my singing and my cooking, as long as I did not speak. As his wife, my role was to listen respectfully when serious subjects were discussed, laugh at his jokes, delight in his amusing tales, and take care of him and our son. Taking care of him did not include sex, but did include cooking, washing, ironing, and cleaning the apartment. In the beginning of our marriage, I wanted to be a good wife. I liked cooking, basically because I like eating, and was proud to modify all my childhood recipes and various Latin recipes with the ingredients I could find in New York. I liked washing but abhorred ironing, and stopped doing it when he demanded that I iron his underwear and pajamas as well as his shirts. As a graduate student with a baby, I had no time for ironing!

"Where are my shorts? I have no underwear," Carlos asked me one morning while I was preparing baby food in the kitchen.

"Look in the bedroom. There is a bunch of clean laundry in the yellow basket."

He disappeared into the bedroom and soon appeared clutching several pairs of his shorts in his hand. "They are not ironed. I cannot wear these."

Another week passed. I did the laundry but not the ironing. Carlos kept complaining about not having underwear.

I had finals. I kept laundering clothes but did not iron. Eventually the finals were over, and one day I decided to be a good wife and iron his underwear. I counted the pairs of shorts as I folded them, ironed. There were forty-eight pairs. Apparently, as the weeks went by, when Carlos could not find ironed pairs, he went out and bought six new pairs. And another six new pairs, and another six new pairs. Smiling, I put them all away on the closet shelf, thinking, *It will now really be some time before I have to iron them again, won't it?* As if I had a dirty (but ironed) secret to keep.

Carlos traveled more and more and stayed longer and longer. Days rolled into each other, and since I had to do everything myself, I had no time to examine or analyze the situation too closely. No time to ponder any potential changes. Carlos would return from a business trip and work late at the office to catch up on things. At dinner he would tune out and excuse himself soon to go read the papers. We slept in separate bedrooms. I listened to Jason's stories and to accounts of his days at nursery school, studied for my classes, and did the housework. Days were busy, the evenings were busy, and the minute my head touched the pillow, I was asleep. Carlos's bags were almost always ready for yet another trip. He would tell me a day or two in advance that he was leaving and how long he would stay.

"Going to Caracas on Tuesday. Do I have clean shirts?"

"How long are you staying?"

"Not sure. A week. Ten days at most."

"Yes, you have enough clean shirts and underwear for a week. Isn't there a place in Caracas to have things laundered?"

"Yes, I'll find something. The hotel is too expensive."

"But you are not staying in hotels, are you?"

"No, not the last time. They put me up in an apartment the company keeps in Caracas."

Carlos would leave with scarcely any information of where he would be staying or for how long. In the beginning I used to ask for a copy of his itinerary, but that got me in trouble with his secretary in New York. If he did not come back on the day he was supposed to, she would call me.

"Carlos has been delayed," I would explain. "His plane was overbooked. He'll be arriving on the next available plane."

When he still didn't arrive, she would call and ask for the actual arrival date and time so she could reschedule the meetings he was missing. Since Carlos did not tell me when he would be back and often stayed days longer than planned, I felt more and more intimidated by his secretary and her calls. More than once she implied that I might be lying. As his wife, wasn't I supposed to know exactly where he was and how long he would be there? Didn't I care when my husband was coming back? Actually, I didn't. But it was too hard to admit to loss of communication and a failing marriage. I wanted to be good at things. I wanted to be a good wife. I wanted to be a good mother. A woman's task was to be a good wife, a good mother.

After a while I realized that Carlos was completely unreliable and had no concept of time. If he promised to call, for instance, on a Wednesday evening, Jason and I would wait up for his call—Jason often falling asleep on the sofa—but his call would never come. And then he would call on Friday.

"Why didn't you call on Wednesday?" I'd ask.

"What do you mean 'on Wednesday'? I could not call on Wednesday. We were in a meeting and later went out for dinner and by the time I was back in the apartment I was too tired to call. Anyway, what difference does it make? I am calling now."

"When are you coming back? Your secretary called again."

"Don't worry. I will call her first thing in the morning."

"It's Saturday."

"Oh, yes, yes. I forgot. Anyway, I am coming back on Sunday."

He was never contrite about his missed calls or missed arrivals. I stopped listening. I stopped caring. Life was easier when he was not home. Less complicated and with less work. Jason and I developed a routine. Once a week, I would not cook dinner and we went to a fish restaurant for grilled grouper, French fries, and salad. On Saturdays we went to the Museum of Natural History, or to the movies, even theater matinees. We would have lunch at Italian restaurants, because, like most children, Jason loved spaghetti. We would read the menus aloud, trying to sound Italian and wondered what *gnocchi* looked and tasted like. We both declined risotto; rice was one of the staples at home. I would order a glass of wine with my meal, and these outings felt as if I had a full social life. Jason was good company.

Thinking back, it is clear that I had entered marriage unprepared and with a bagful of misconceptions. I was not in love with Carlos and dated him out of loneliness and in order not to feel out of place, still a foreigner. It was flattering to date a man who was so much older and experienced. He seemed complete, not ill defined, as I felt most of the time. What I perceived as maturity and confidence later revealed themselves as single-mindedness and inflexibility. Still a bachelor and living alone at thirty-seven, he was so used to making decisions for himself, it never occurred to him to ask for my opinion. And I let him, because it eased my confusion at having to navigate through numerous options of my new life. There were so many new rules to keep in mind, necessary to keep me from doing anything out of sync with the rest of people. Glad to be saved from making important decisions, I was content with my immediate domains of wife, mother, and a graduate student.

Carlos managed the finances, selected the health insurance, his pension plan, and made decision about major purchases, such as furniture and the car. But he did not always trust his judgment and sought the advice of salespeople when buying the most innocuous items, be it food or clothing. I preferred to investigate before buying. I take time to think and gather information from objective sources before forming an opinion. I was also especially distrustful of any advice given by a salesman. To my mind, they were only interested in selling me something and making a profit. Carlos nevertheless distrusted my choices, thought them formulated in haste, and vacillated about agreeing with me. That was probably his way of preserving his dominance and control.

Carlos worked during the day, often met his male friends in the evening or on weekends, and read newspapers when at home. He did not like television, but he would eagerly watch tennis and soccer games whenever possible. Actually, his interest in sports was limited to watching soccer and tennis. He did not participate. Until Jason was old enough to play basketball, we never went to a ball game. But Carlos could name many soccer players, especially those from South America, and how many goals they had scored against which team and in which games; and the rankings of the top tennis players. Soccer did not interest me, possibly because one of my high school teachers of literature once described it as “a bunch of illiterates chasing a piece of stinky leather to exhaustion.” I could never get that image out of my mind. Tennis, on the other hand, was just boring. I preferred regular television, and gradually grew less and less annoyed with commercials.

In the evenings, when Jason was asleep and Carlos not at home, I dreamed about making my own documentaries. I would jot down topics for my imagined future articles and list the people I would interview. If I had time, I even started researching some topics and made copious notes.

Not surprisingly, I was especially intrigued by the status of women. Betty Friedan had just published *The Feminine Mystique*, inspiring a new wave of American feminism.

I could easily support feminism, especially as a campaign for women's rights to vote, to earn a wage equal to a man's in a similar job, and to own property. I sympathized with the women's suffrage movements of the nineteenth and early twentieth century. I admired women such as Susan B. Anthony, who campaigned for the abolition of slavery and women's right to vote. But it was hard to understand why it took until 1920 and the passage of the Nineteenth Amendment of the United States Constitution to grant women the right to vote in all states. In the Soviet Union after the October Revolution, and in Yugoslavia and other east European countries, as well as in China and Cuba and other countries, after World War II the Communist Party granted women the right to vote and integrated women into the workforce. Discrimination based on gender became illegal, and women were granted equality in education, marriage, careers, and various other legal rights. During World War II, women fought against Nazis alongside men, and continued to be politically active after the war.

I reread some of Simone de Beauvoir's writings, but failed to agree with her ideas about fluidity of sex and sexual attitudes, except for a woman's right to dictate what happened to her body. Therefore, she had the right to terminate unwanted pregnancies and the right to birth control. Having grown up in a socialist country, I didn't see the need for feminism. In my former country, there were many women doctors. Quite a few of my teachers in school had been men. Several of our well-regarded poets were women. I could not remember knowing any women lawyers, but two of my best friends from high school became lawyers. There were several policewomen in my hometown. The electrician in my high school was a woman.

Gender should not prevent a person from choosing a certain profession. And a woman's profession should not prevent her from being a good wife and a mother. Pursuing a career could only enhance an individual's personal worth, making him or her a more interesting partner. I failed to perceive any hidden sexist power structures. Of course women were as smart or as stupid as men, and as capable of entering any profession. And of course they had equal opportunities. That I wanted to be a good wife was founded on the notion that it was positive to want to please the man you loved and married. I saw absolutely no conflict between being a good wife and mother and a good journalist. The idea was to strive to be the best at everything one did. My identity seemed solid. Feminism as a movement seemed superfluous. Not everything had to be politicized. Nevertheless, I set out to investigate why it was necessary in my new country. I needed to better understand the complexity of conflicts that were driving feminism.

I could sympathize with Betty Friedan's early Marxism, but thought that her abandonment of a PhD and academic career influenced her emphasis on the unfulfilling and stifling full-time homemaker role. I could not accept the restricted and suppressed view of a suburban wife and mother, who felt trapped and imprisoned by her motherhood. I failed to see the need for consciousness-raising sessions. What I easily saw as injustice, however, was the unequal place of women at work and the need for major legislative changes for equal employment opportunities and affirmative action.

There was acute need for child-care changes. In order for a woman to have a profession and pursue a career, family planning was essential, and some division of labor within marriage was critical. A marriage ought to be a collaborative effort in all respects, a team-work with equal distribution of chores. My marriage, obviously, was not that. The promised self-sufficiency of feminism could boost a woman's confidence and support her autonomy as a person—until she fell in love with a man. Once in love, another dynamic arose. You had a sudden desire to be loved in return, but also to please your man. You became comfortable within a cocoon of submissiveness as long as you perceived him to be deserving of this personal sacrifice. With time a degree of hypocrisy took residence within your soul as you failed to distinguish between your natural sexuality and gender from that constructed by society. Resisting this change provoked irritation, which grew into anxiety if the object of your love demanded more and more of your personal sacrifice and gave less and less in return.

Having experienced marriage and motherhood, I sympathized with Friedan's critique of the entrenched societal order, but I was not yet fully aware of the obstacles and pitfalls of trying to compete professionally with men. The struggle for equality within the workplace was yet to come, so I viewed the initial debates between Betty Friedan and Gloria Steinem with suspicion. Gloria was an attractive young woman about to enter a career in journalism, unencumbered with family obligations. In my mind she was not capable of understanding that a woman might wish for it all, the marriage, the family, and a successful career.

I set out to research and understand why socialism permitted professional equality and why capitalism, with its multitude of choices, seemed to curtail the progress of women. I was going to interview women in different countries, spanning a variety of subjects, from their thoughts on motherhood, sex, cooking, friendships with other women and men, hobbies, music choices, clothing preferences, and their professional lives, and write a doctoral dissertation based on this research.

Just thinking and planning this course of action filled me with accomplishment, proud that I found a timely topic of interest. These thoughts were inspirational but yet unformed. Motherhood was not a chore for me, and aspiring to be a good mother and a good wife should not incapacitate me from being a good writer or a successful journalist. It was a bit difficult to imagine Carlos with an apron and mixing a salad, but I had seen my father with Jason. It was my father who had taught me how to hold him, how to bathe him, how to change his diaper. Yes, it helped that my father was a physician, but his profession never made him less of a man. It must be insecurity, I decided, that prevented men from doing housework or caring for children—the same insecurity that made them poor husbands.

It had to be a societal illness stemming from insecurity that kept men from paying equal salaries to women and that allowed them to prevent women from holding office, and pushing their daughters to be teachers and nurses, not physicians or lawyers or engineers or journalists. Did it all stem from insecurity, men's need to grip power so tightly in their fists?

During the long evenings when Carlos was away and Jason fell asleep in my lap while I studied, I would jot down thoughts about the questions for my dissertation interviews, even though I had not yet approached any of my professors with the idea and did not have a formal thesis advisor. Jason once woke up as I carried him to bed.

"You are smiling, Mom," he said sleepily. "Something you read?"

I kissed him and whispered, "Good night," so his dreams would continue uninterrupted. And then I continued to dream mine.

Three

I TOOK COURSES IN journalism, although it seemed unlikely I would practice it much. I also took courses in film theory and in cinematic techniques in preparation to participate in TV journalism. The class schedule was convenient and fit nicely with my babysitting schedule. My mother babysat in the mornings. Jason had to be taken to her house and later fetched. Carlos could take him in the mornings, and I would bring him home. Later, when Jason started nursery school, it was easier for me to take courses in the morning again, thus increasing the credits I was earning toward my degree.

Both film courses were taught by Will, a charismatic and gifted teacher who made us believe that making films was the reason to live.

"Films are made for the audience," he would say. "Everything in film is designed for the mind of the audience."

"Journalism," he would continue, "is about information. Nine out of ten people will prefer seeing things than just reading about them. Film is capable of storing and communicating a great amount of information. In an instant it presents a scene that would require pages of prose to describe. Cinematic techniques are methods used by filmmakers not only to entertain, but to provoke a specific emotional response, convey meaning, tell a story.

"In order to engage the audience, the person making films must be a dedicated professional. The best story will fail if the person handling the camera misuses the view, the angle and the movement of the camera."

He discouraged handheld shots, though he acknowledged they could give an impression of immediacy. A tripod was the more professional choice.

He talked about background lighting, cameo lighting, and stage lighting. An entire section of the course was devoted to editing. And of course, there was a long section dedicated to sound. We learned about diegetic or actual sound and non-diegetic sound. We learned about special effects. In his own work, which was mostly documentaries, he experimented with different techniques and asked us to be in his films as subjects and as assistants. He shot a longish video of me talking about my childhood. He kept telling me that a smart person like me could do anything. Why was I so shy? I tried to explain about the thoughts in my head and their complexity versus the imperfect language I had to render them in. He seemed fascinated with my linguistic problems and got more and more interested in me. He kept filming more interviews with me as a subject. As our collaboration grew and I assisted him with other short films he was making, Will asked for my ideas in editing, deleting scenes, rearranging sequences. His topics spanned a range of social issues and a great variety of subjects. As time went on, he increasingly sought out my opinion. I was enormously pleased with the extent of our collaboration and proud when he kept repeating that he had never had a more knowledgeable editing assistant. He valued my judgment, and bit by bit I outgrew my shyness, expressed myself more freely, and felt confident enough even to argue with him.

"Films are not just entertainment, they are art!" Will exclaimed.

"Art as representation of reality or art as expression of the artist?" I dared to ask.

"Art as interpretation. Events have no meaning without interpretation. Facts have no meaning without interpretation. Bare reality is insufficient."

"But, Will, there are different film genres. Some can be pretty abstract or fictional and therefore far removed from any reality. Some, in their interpretation of reality, may be a premeditated alteration of reality. Others are part of journalistic intention to just present events and facts as they occurred—specifically without much commentary. Pure reporting. There are educational films and documentaries."

We spent more and more time together, and I grew less lonely during Carlos's absences and felt a more involved mother with Jason. When I took Jason to the movies, I would point out some aspects of the film technology, but actually, this was more for my benefit than Jason's. Jason, too young to appreciate the technical aspects of filmmaking, was invariably bored with such conversations and steered me back to the content of the movie or his additions and changes to the plot.

Will was an attractive man. Tall and well built, he had presence. His blue eyes shone with palpable emotion and uncommon resolve when he spoke and, especially, when he lectured. His face, framed by a dark beard, exuded raw passion, projecting it into the space that would collapse to include just the two of you. You felt he was talking to you and only you; there was no one else within the suddenly shrunken universe—a trite concept, but nevertheless present and true when Will talked. He was one of the most popular teachers at the university, praised for his innovation in film techniques. No subject was immune from him. Despite his preference for film as art, he made several well-received instructional films and wrote a textbook on the psychology of filmmaking.

An engaging and charismatic teacher, Will stood in front of the class as if on a stage and took evident pride in his performance. We all did feel that it was a performance staged for us. No, not true. Not staged for us, but staged for me ... and me ... and me. Everybody felt each lecture was specifically prepared for him or her. His lectures were well organized but seemed spontaneous, as if each example was plucked out of his memory at that very moment because it was pertinent. He told us humorous personal stories and gave numerous examples to elucidate points that reinforced the general idea of his lectures. He asked questions, and if no one answered them, he would answer them himself. And, of course, he loved visual effects and showed us short and long films, pointing out aspects to remember.

He would show a scene taken from a low camera angle in which the subject seemed threatening, powerful, and dominant; and then a high-angle shot of the same person, who now appeared vulnerable, small, inconsequential. He pointed out scenes shot with flood lighting and indicated how and when to achieve a subtle "Rembrandt" effect. He differentiated between single and panoramic shots.

"The basic property of film is photographic. The single shot is the film's basic building block. Through a calculated structuring and interaction of shots, a film will create meaning and shape the mental processes of the spectator, the audience. "

"Panoramic shot," Will continued, "can have multiple effects. In one scene it can describe a landscape, while in another it can follow a moving train or an animal running through the forest. It can also imitate the direction of a dialogue. Panoramic movement creates meaning by separation from the static modes of photography. Single shots are similar to the discrete notes in a piece of music, which are shaped by the composer into melodies. But for a piece of music to give a total experience, the feeling of the whole, it must be rich in tones and overtones. So does film editing make a film from good single shots, which to begin with are mere shards of reality. Good editing turns them into truth or deceit. Good editing may start a train of ideas and give them a determined direction. Good editing will interpret."

To Will, film and television were equally important media. We watched Dick Cavett and Barbara Walters interviews again and again. Walters's interview with Fidel Castro was one of his favorites.

"Interviews must be informative," he said, "but let the audience be the judge. Always think of the audience. Never, never, forget the audience."

He cautioned over and over again to think of the audience, of who might be watching the interview and not just about the celebrity who was being interviewed.

"The interviews must not be about issues, but about people. How they are affected by those issues and how successfully or unsuccessfully they have dealt with them."

He was fond of saying that everybody had interesting events in their lives, but what was interesting to one person might not be so interesting to his neighbor.

"You have to keep the audience in mind at all times and must never bore the audience. Do ask personal questions, because they are always people in the audience who think that what celebrities eat for breakfast is important. Get the celebrity to explain in simple language those things he or she is famous for. Ask actors how they prepare for a role, how much they prepare for it. Ask scientists to explain what they study not only in the language they habitually use, but to explain in simple terms why the study of this minuscule part of nature touches them personally, what in their scientific pursuit is relevant to our pedestrian existence. Bring them to the level of the audience. Ask the politicians who their role models are and who they think they resemble. And yes, ask the celebrities about their personal lives, about something innocuous that will bring them down to everyman's level of existence."

We had mock interviews, taking turns being the interviewee and the interviewer. Will videotaped these and then indicated our strong points and when we did not succeed. His criticism was always clear and constructive. If he felt it necessary, he made us repeat the interview again immediately, before it slipped out of mind, to banish the unsuccessful one from memory and substitute it with the more successful version.

Most people avoid being criticized, but Will's suggestions

always improved the outcome and were tolerated without a single complaint.

As his assistants, we were required to speak to the class about our individual projects or the one we were doing with him. In the beginning I was shy, and when I had to speak in front of others, I was acutely aware of my accent and pedantic in my choice of words. In my head I was translating from my native tongue into English, instead of trying to think in English and discarding the translation safety net. My presentation came out stilted and forced, because I was always watching myself and trying hard not to say or do the wrong thing. Sweat would pour from my armpits and down along my ribs, and I would hope that nobody noticed. I would take great care in dressing every morning before class, choosing clothes that would not show if I sweated. I never wore just a shirt but always added a sweater or jacket no matter how hot it was, petrified that my wet armpits would betray my anxiety. Some days the perspiration stains were the only thing on my mind, and I could hardly concentrate on anything else as I tried to hide my embarrassment and the ugly wet armpits. There were no antiperspirants that I did not try, but I hated their smell, which, unfortunately, was another telltale sign of my discomfort.

Shyness is very restrictive and totally self-imposed. A shy person lives in a self-imposed prison, walled in by attitudes and beliefs that are seldom based on evidence.

With Will's patient and gentle suggestions on how to improve my pronunciation or how to move more gracefully, and with the approval I would see in his eyes, I steadily built the courage to be more spontaneous. It was all right if I did not plan everything to the last *T*; it was all right if things had to change direction in the middle of the course. I slowly built confidence, trusting myself to explain what I wanted to say, even if I did not do it in the first sentence. It was all right to say, "Sorry, let me start again."

Will made me aware of my surroundings, of little imperfections in daily life that tumbled unexpectedly into our paths all the time. I did not have to control every single moment. It was all right to be focused and concentrated, just as much as it was all right to be spontaneous. Life needed both, a balance.

As Will made me more relaxed, I became aware of everything else, apart from my anxiety and wet armpits. By the end of the semester, I was wearing shirts without sweaters or jackets. Still, I fretted about social occasions with strangers and although invited often to parties, I found excuses not to go.

That was just as well since Jason provided a lot of entertainment at home. If Carlos was traveling, Jason occupied my spare time. And coming home to him felt right. Being with Jason felt right. And at home with Jason, I had no fears of speaking or performing. At home I never fretted about wet stains at my armpits. At home there was no awkwardness. With Jason, conversation came naturally and did not need to be translated. My thoughts and emotions could pour out uncensored.

When I worked with Will on one of his projects, it was clear that he knew exactly what he wanted to achieve, but he nevertheless asked for my opinions and suggestions. He listened to them, concentrating, with a deep furrow in his brow and his intense blue eyes fixed on me, as if he wanted to reach the depths of what I was saying, very careful not to misunderstand. He let me talk, sometimes for great lengths of time, without interruption. When I finished he would keep looking at me with the same intensity, and then smile and say, "Alexandra, this is a magnificent idea. I have never had an assistant with such profound knowledge and such capacity to argue the point."

Delighted by his praise, I believed every word, and the next time tried to be even more ingenious, more creative. Magically, my ideas often became part of the solution to a problem. He did this not only with me. He had a talent to be inclusive of everybody's ideas. Like a good architect, he used materials of not the prime quality, but in places where they stood out and improved the whole. He built a masterpiece with the bricks each of us provided, a whole that was truly more than each part, although each of us could clearly identify the brick we had handed him. This inclusiveness made us feel important. His democratic ways allowed each of us to identify with the whole and be proud of the final achievement. If pressed we would have to admit that if we'd been on our own, the scene would not have worked. We needed Will's input.

There was no doubt in my mind that Will was a genius, and he let his talents rub on everybody around him. He shared his intellect, his creativity, his knowledge generously, and somehow I felt smarter in his presence. I became more creative, more inventive, drawn to this challenge of achieving something extraordinary and not just an everyday, half-baked thing. His presence mandated intellectual endeavor, urging me to find answers to problems. I was often astonished with their simplicity.

Success in problem solving can be addictive. If one is motivated enough to find the answer, nothing else matters. This blind dedication can be detrimental to relationships, meal habits, and sleep habits, because until a solution is found, nothing else matters.

Since Carlos was on business trips so often and my mother offered to babysit Jason, I could indulge in this activity fully. When a project was satisfactorily brought to completion, my satisfaction was beyond any rewards I had known before. I felt a mix of pride, of belonging to a group, and a sense that anything else was now possible.

With each successful project with Will, I noticed a new freedom and a new confidence that, yes, I could do this. Yes, I could speak the language everybody understood, despite my accent, and yes, I could speak to an audience. I had things to say.

We eventually slept together. On a cold and rainy night, Will offered me a ride home. Since Carlos was abroad and Jason at my mother's, I asked him to the apartment for a cup of tea. Whenever Carlos was out of town and I had classes, my mother gladly kept Jason at her house longer, so the rides home became a habit. We chatted effortlessly, and at one point I confessed my feelings about him as a teacher.

"You know," I said, "I have learned a lot from you. You are easily the best teacher I ever had."

"You are a good student. But there are things I have learned from you."

"Oh, really? What things? How to use the wrong words or stammer?" I teased.

"No, no. About people. About other countries, their customs. How different simple things can be if you are raised in another culture. What an emotional toll you paid to adjust to being here. You made me aware of certain behaviors to such a degree that I started noticing discrepancies, gradations ... I am more aware of my own actions now, since I've listened to you complain about being unsure about yours. I have become more introspective."

"Introspection helps, but can be dangerous."

"I don't see why."

"Well, it may result in learning things about oneself that may not be easy to accept."

"True." He paused. "Such as the fact that one is falling in love with a student?"

"Or ... that one is falling in love with a teacher, while one is married?"

My apartment was next to a church. As we made love for the first time, the church bells started ringing, the world chiming in. We laughed at this auspicious start of our relationship. The universe approved!

Will contemplated making a film with Leon Festinger's idea of cognitive dissonance as the central theme. We selected the psychology texts, read them together, discussed them, planned scenes, made love. Discussed scenes, planned their sequence, made love.

Alone at home I took care of Jason, happier than ever before, completely fulfilled as a mother, as a woman. Soon Will and I spent all our available free time together.

Will would undress me slowly, piece by piece, murmuring endearments as he revealed my body.

"What beautiful skin you have," he would whisper. "I want to touch every inch of it, every part. How could anyone resist such beauty? I'm prisoner of love. I love your body, your eyes ..." He spilled kisses over my face, "Your lips, your hair. You are perfection. I am home."

None of his lovemaking suggestions felt embarrassing. It was all quite natural, the natural evolution of our relationship. I walked around naked, feeling totally at ease. Will's hand sculpted my body into this perfect piece of art. How could I resist feeling beautiful? At the same time, with each minute we spent together I felt I was becoming more beautiful. I stopped wearing a bra. My breasts were small and it probably made no difference whether I wore one or not. I looked for clothing made of materials that would cling sensually to my new body, loving the touch of the fabric over each microscopic part of my skin as I moved, as I walked, and as I danced alone around my empty apartment, entranced by the memory of his hands and his touch. We listened to music a lot, especially the Beatles, but never had a real opportunity to dance. I imagined Will was a good dancer and dreamed of dancing with him, held tight in slow, sensuous movement, lost in each other's embrace.

Will's talented hands created this new enchanting person, this woman, me! Delighted beyond belief, that Will not only had shaped a new sensual woman, but that he had also freed the rational being, a professional persona, I could be proud of. He sculpted a new Alexandra, a happy Alexandra. And I soon realized, an Alexandra who was a better mother to Jason. I became more patient and took time to explain things to Jason. I played with him more often and engaged in fanciful narratives, taking us to Mars or having us fly over Manhattan looking for all the little boys and girls who still were not sleeping at nine o'clock at night, Jason's bedtime. Jason invariably found a few still awake and begged to stay up a little longer.

What I still remember most vividly about Will—after so many years—is his voice. His breathless whisper, the endearments he whispered into my ear, his rushed intake of breath, a small sigh, and a delicate lisp, a tiny percussion sound as if of clearing a wayward facial hair from his lips. His private voice, his whisper of love and longing. And I remember his defensive smile when I caught him in some mischief. His vibrant personality helped him get away with a lot of mischief, a lot of teasing, which he accompanied with that unforgettable smile. I kept dreaming of hearing his voice much longer than anything else about him. The special way he pronounced my name, as if I was compelled to discover this quality of mine for the first time, my name, pronounced with love and always, I thought, with thinly veiled longing.

Once we got hot dogs and a salad that contained lettuce, shredded carrots, and cabbage. For some reason that I no longer remember, I complained about eating raw cabbage. Will took a forkful and stuffed it into his mouth.

"How can you not like it?" he asked. "It is crunchy. Don't you like crunchy?" He wore his familiar mischievous grin, teasing me, his smile mocking my reluctance to eat the crunchy salad.

Many of our conversations were playful, mocking, and irresistibly good-natured. Life was lighthearted, easygoing, cheerful, and fun ... with Will. It is possible that he hid problems he experienced in his life apart from me. When together, life had a curious lightness. It was bereft of shadows or dreariness or gloom, a life without substance, perhaps as in a vacuum. A vacuum created by love, devoid of complexities, dirty tricks, manipulations, or any of those games two people are forced to play when out of love.

As he was about to tell me something deeply felt, his face would reveal the briefest of preparations, small lisps, similar to the movements of tiny wings, beating with a faster and faster rhythm, until the words came out, softly caressing, the wings now calm, his lips ready for a kiss. When he called on the phone, my surroundings faded at the sound of his voice. All was just the voice emanating from the instrument, softly enticing, seductive, and full of promise and love.

Will was soon spending all his free time with Jason and me whenever Carlos was out of town. With a video camera that hardly ever left his hand, Will videotaped our trips to the Bronx Zoo, Fire Island, eating messy hot dogs, faces smeared with mustard and ketchup. These moments were stolen from life and made our own. Jason laughed at Will's preposterous, fantastic stories, invented on the spot, and teased him about ketchup on his beard. At the zoo Jason wanted to know why we had to look at snakes in the dark, and Will explained their nocturnal habits, teaching Jason a new word—nocturnal. At home Jason kept repeating it like a chant, delighting in its sound.

Will drove a BMW with beige upholstery, a definite improvement over our Volkswagen Beetle. He was proud of his car, although he'd bought it used, and even more proud that he'd successfully bargained down the price. It sat majestically on the road, and I felt safe within its beige interior.

I planned to tell Carlos at the first opportunity that I had fallen in love with another man and wanted a divorce. But between his travels, my schoolwork, caring for Jason, the time never seemed right.

Will was reticent about his private life and seldom talked about his family. Some information would sneak out unintentionally, and if pressed for more, he would change the subject. Bit by bit I learned that he was the oldest child and had two brothers and a sister. His mother seemed to have curtailed his childhood. He would reluctantly describe his first job as a newspaper boy, of selling magazines door to door, and of delivering laundry. Or of how his mother sent him to buy things at the store when he was barely six years old. Sometimes he spoke wistfully, sometimes with pride that he had been asked to act more like a father than a brother to his siblings. He would on occasion complain about his mother and her controlling behavior, but seldom talked about his mostly absent father. Apparently his father fancied himself an attractive man and spent more time in bars than at home. His father never established himself in a profession. When Will was a child, his father was a reluctant barber for a short period of time. At other times he repaired appliances, refinished furniture, and even tuned pianos. He changed jobs many times and was frequently unemployed. Both his parents were poorly educated; neither had finished high school. I did not dare ask prying questions, since the topic made Will anxious and unwilling to talk about his family anymore.

Will, however, proudly talked about his high school years. Smart, extroverted, tall, and good-looking, he was elected captain of whichever team he joined and was voted most popular boy in the senior class. He had lots of friends and once told me he preferred being friends with girls rather than boys, because girls were less threatening and less competitive.

One of Will's classmates later became a famous social psychologist who studied blind obedience to authority, investigating to what degree it could happen in a democratic society. They were close friends, and when he was older, Will's documentaries often explored similar subjects.

Will was always protective of his much younger sister,

Olivia. She was a sickly child, spending long periods of time in the hospital. When she was five or six, she spent half a year in the hospital with virulent pneumonia. Her health remained an issue, but Will was not forthcoming about any details. One of his brothers was a musician; he played in a rock band and was often on the road. The other brother was married with children and lived in Arizona.

I never had a chance to meet any of his family. Well, once I almost met his father when he came to visit Will at the university. I had taken the elevator to Will's floor, and as I got off, an older man got on. The elevator doors closed, and I barely had the time to smile at the man who for some reason seemed familiar, reminded me of someone I thought I knew.

"Was that your father?" I asked Will.

"Yes. It was my father." Will seemed annoyed with the visit and refused to talk about it.

Will's office was not large. He was still at the beginning of his academic career, an assistant professor. The office was cluttered with camera equipment, photographs, magazines, newspapers, and books. Some photos of sport events, showing a younger Will, were framed on the wall, while others were scattered on the shelf of a bookcase that ran along one wall, propped up by the books. Will once mentioned that he had been a track-and-field star in high school. He even showed me cinder fragments still in his knee. The scrapes were long healed, but he was nostalgically proud of his injury. Nearly hidden by books and photographs was a small wood sculpture of a peasant girl with what looked like a sheaf of wheat in her arm. One entire bookshelf had clocks. Not enough to be considered a true collection, but enough to be a frequent topic of conversations whenever someone entered his office for the first time. When I asked him whether he collected clocks, he answered, "No, not really."

"It looks to me as if you do. There are at least"—I started counting them—"thirteen, fourteen, fifteen. Fifteen clocks? Not a collector?"

"No, I don't collect clocks. A student once came to an appointment with me ten minutes late. I told him he was late. He said that his class had been dismissed late and it was not his fault. I insisted that he was late nevertheless. We argued about the significance and perception of time for more than an hour, totally forgetting the reason he was supposed to be meeting with me. So we had to reschedule his appointment, because he had to go to his next class. At our next meeting he gave me a clock—an instrument to measure time—as a present. Soon other students were giving me clocks. He must have told them that I liked clocks. And actually, I do like clocks. Time is of importance, isn't it?"

When Will wasn't talking about film or photography, he talked about the relativity of time, one of his favorite subjects. When he did not have a camera in his hand, he held a book. His reading interests were diverse and eclectic. In addition to our discussions about films, we sometimes discussed plays and novels, but I was surprised by his taste in poetry. I remember that he liked William Carlos Williams, and that his favorite poet was one I had never heard of, Harold Norse. I am not sure, but they may have been friends in college, or someone Will knew had been in school with Norse. I never got it right, except that there was a personal connection. English and American poetry was difficult for me. I liked haiku, probably because it was short and to the point. My favorite one was about a butterfly sitting on a bell—until it rang. I do not remember who wrote it, perhaps an anonymous Japanese, and if it really sounded like that. The idea, the image of the butterfly sitting on a bell, though, remains vividly in my mind even now.

Once when Will was late for our meeting and arrived uncharacteristically angry and exasperated, I asked what was wrong. He blurted out that he was done with therapy.

"Therapy? You are in therapy?" I asked, surprised. He never seemed in need of therapy to me. Patient, calm, collected, and almost always in a cheerful and playful mood, he was the last person I would have thought needed therapy.

"Well, yes. Isn't everybody?"

"No, not everybody ..." I replied in doubt.

Did I actually know anyone who was in therapy? Yes, I had heard that a friend of a friend, who tried to commit suicide, was taken to Bellevue Hospital and given shock therapy. Will seemed far from ever being depressed or a candidate for suicide, and certainly not for shock therapy.

"Why are you in therapy? What kind of therapy?"

He ignored my questions and started criticizing his therapist. "George thinks I need to come more often."

"Who is George?"

"My therapist. I told him about us, that I was in love with you. And he said that you were a bad influence."

"A bad influence? How? Why? Because I am married?"

"George thinks that I am not being honest with myself. This is bullshit! I have never been more honest about anything! No, no, it has nothing to do with you being married, my love. He is just so wrong about our relationship!"

I was perplexed and understood nothing. But Will was not willing to discuss it any further. Eventually, I learned that his therapy had to do with a suicide after all, but not Will's. Will had a gay friend in college who committed suicide. Apparently all of the man's friends were urged to see a therapist. At least that was what Will told me.

Perhaps it was inevitable that I would get pregnant again. Will and I agreed that it was not the best of times to have a baby, and I started looking for means to end the pregnancy. A friend of a friend of my mother's recommended a Hungarian gynecologist who had an office on Long Island. Will agreed to drive me there and loaned me part of the money I needed for this illegal—at that time—procedure. I did not think too much about the consequences, convinced that the termination of this unwanted pregnancy was my only choice. I was young, had a son, believed it was easy to get pregnant, and thought that if I wanted to get pregnant again in the future, there would be no problem. Having a child with Will was something to be considered and done at a future, more opportune time. Will was supportive of the termination and did not at all argue against it. His explanation had to do with his work and imminent projects and anticipated travel in respect to such plans.

Carlos was away on one of his business trips. I got up in the morning, took Jason to preschool, and waited for Will to drive me to Long Island. The doctor's office was easy to find. Will stayed in the car. There were no other patients in the waiting room. I was expected; my mother's friend had made the appointment for me. The receptionist ushered me into the office immediately. The doctor, dressed in a crisp white coat, shook my hand. He was a tall, burly man, well past middle age. He wore glasses that sat low on his nose and peered at me above them. He had a comforting demeanor. In a strong Hungarian accent, he asked about my mother and her friends, and we chatted pleasantly about politics in Hungary and Hungarian food.

"Do you ever make goulash?" he asked.

"Yes, often. And chicken paprikash. But don't like to make palacsintas," I said. "My mother makes them often. When my sister was small, she was a finicky eater. She really liked them, and I think we ate them every day after lunch for almost two years."

"I like them with walnuts," the doctor said.

"I like them with prune preserves."

He smiled, surprised. "I don't think I ever tasted that!"

"My mother sometimes bakes them filled with cottage cheese."

"Yes, we did that at home too." In the same breath, he became serious and asked, "So are you ready for the procedure? You really want to do this, terminate the pregnancy?"

"Yes, I do."

In another part of the office, the nurse asked for the money, took the envelope of cash I had brought, and told me to undress below the waist. The doctor came in and in unhurried, clear language explained what he was going to do. While he put on gloves, he told the nurse which instruments he was going to use. He then gave me an injection of an antibiotic, another of an anesthetic, and proceeded with the dilatation and curettage. I did not feel much discomfort, and sooner than I thought it would be over, it was over. The whole event was utterly unremarkable, similar to so many other visits to a gynecologist—slight embarrassment at being examined, slight discomfort in having to accommodate a speculum, slight discomfort in the rest of the procedure—a normal, common thing we women went through on a regular basis. Maybe just a bit more painful, but totally unremarkable. How easy it was to stop being pregnant; how easy to eliminate this unwanted occurrence. How easy to proceed with life unencumbered by the need to plan for a place in the world for another child.

Thinking back, I am horrified at my eagerness to terminate this unwanted pregnancy, brought on by a desire to eliminate any further complications in my and Will's already complicated lives. But at the time I had no second thoughts.

"That's it," the doctor said. "You may have some bleeding for a day or two. If it becomes severe with a lot of pain, come back to the office."

And then he added, looking into my eyes, in a measured, firm voice, "Do not call on the phone. Just come back. Okay?"

"Yes, Doctor, I understand." Abortions were illegal, and I had no intention of getting him into any trouble.

Will drove me home, gave me a hug and kiss, and left. My mother promised to keep Jason overnight. I was home alone. I went to the bedroom to lie down and rest, mindful of the doctor's warning about not provoking a bleeding.

In the apartment on the floor above us lived an older couple I did not know well. They had no children and lived alone. We occasionally exchanged greetings in the elevator.

They seemed friendly, especially if I was with Jason. They always engaged him in conversation, wanting to know whether he liked playing in the park or if he had a special friend in school. When Carlos was with us, they avoided looking at any of us and remained silent. The man was thin, tall, and stooped. I don't think he shaved regularly, because he always had a day-old gray beard. Even during relatively warm weather, he wore gloves as if he needed to hide his hands. The woman was much shorter and just as thin. They were both pale and appeared undernourished, by food and by life, a history of disappointments evident in their postures. She carried a look of perpetual doubt on her wrinkled face. Her entire face reminded me of a rhetorical question. Her clothes were worn and shabby. A woolen red scarf was her constant companion, a bit too long, I thought.

I wondered about the pair of them, because I could hear them arguing often and loudly. I could not understand what they were saying, but their tones of voice left no doubt that they were in disagreement. Sometimes there was a thud, as if a body had fallen. Sometimes I heard furniture being moved. Carlos ignored these noises when he was home, and if I mentioned them, he speculated about their drinking problems.

After the visit to the Hungarian gynecologist, I lay down on my bed and soon fell asleep. A loud thud from above woke me up. I looked at the clock on my night table. I had not slept long; it was still early afternoon. Judging by the sound from the apartment above mine, I was sure somebody had fallen. But given the history of such disturbances, I thought nothing of it and went back to sleep. Then I was awakened again, this time by my doorbell, which was chiming repeatedly and insistently. Then someone actually banged on my apartment door, and the bell chimed again. I got up cautiously and went to the door. I had no particular desire to open it.

"Who is it?" I called.

"Police. Open the door!"

Police? Suddenly I was petrified. How did they know about my abortion? Was the Hungarian doctor in trouble? Would I go to jail? Would my mother be able to take care of Jason? What explanation would I give to Carlos? I had never told him I was pregnant. Should I claim that the baby was his? Should I call Will? Should I deny everything? I frantically looked for my robe, grabbed it, and opened the door, still in my nightgown and slippers with a robe thrown around my shoulders.

"Ma'am, we are very sorry for disturbing you," apologized a young, handsome policeman.

"Can we come in and use your fire escape?" asked a second policeman. As he came closer, I saw he carried a heavy wrench and a crowbar.

"I'm sorry," I said. "I did not hear the bell. I was in the bedroom, sleeping. I have a cold."

I tried to give a plausible reason for being in bed in the middle of the afternoon, but the policeman with the wrench could not have cared less about me. He hurried to my living room window, opened it, and climbed out on the fire escape.

"Ma'am," the handsome one said, "this is an emergency. We need access to the apartment above you. We are very glad you were home to let us in and onto the fire escape."

Collecting myself as I realized I was not the target of their emergency, I asked about what had happened. But by then both policemen were already out the window and climbing to the floor above. Looking out after them, I saw them struggle to open the window of the older couple's apartment. After some difficulty they got it open and disappeared into the apartment. It was winter and, feeling the chill, I tightened my robe more snugly around me. By now there was a commotion outside my apartment door, which had remained opened. A group of my neighbors stood there noisily exchanging comments about the nature of police emergency.

"The husband came home drunk and realized he locked himself out of the apartment," said one of my neighbors. "He banged on the door but his wife didn't hear him. He made so much noise that any of his neighbors who were home came out of their apartments to find out what was going on. I told him to call his wife on the phone."

"He called several times from my apartment," one woman said, "but there was no answer."

The man continued. "He said his wife was in the apartment, but nobody believed him because he was drunk. They thought his wife probably went out on some errands. He told me to call the police." The man shrugged. "So I did."

Calmed down by the explanations, I retreated to my apartment and sat on the sofa, shivering because my living room window remained open. As I considered if I could close it, the younger officer reappeared on my fire escape and stepped back through the window. I must have still looked perplexed and somewhat frightened, because he sat on the sofa and patted my hand.

"Ma'am, don't worry. Everything is fine. Thank you so much for your help. Without access to the fire escape, we wouldn't have been able to enter the apartment above. Lucky you were home! We tried other apartments on the lower floors, but everybody else was at work. You should go back to bed. You look a little under the weather."

"So what happened? Was the lady at home?" I asked. I still hadn't gotten over my shock at seeing the police at my door after I'd just broken the law.

"Oh, yes. The lady. She was home. We found her on the floor. It looks she had a stroke or something. We called the ambulance."

Even as he spoke we could hear approaching sirens. The policeman rose to go.

"I have to go now, ma'am. You take care. Bye!" And he was gone.

I went to the window, looked up, saw no one else on the fire escape, and closed the window. The commotion outside my door subsided, the neighbors had dispersed, and I shut the door. I went to my bedroom, too agitated, too excited by the events, and not yet fully comprehending what had just happened. And, yes, I felt enormous relief at not being the target of the emergency ... at not being found out.

The rest of my recovery was, I think, that much faster due to this encounter with the police. For a while I wasn't sure whether the old lady's stroke—from which she did not recover—really happened. But it must have, because there was talk of a funeral I did not go to and I no longer met her husband in the elevator. He moved out. Soon after a young couple rented the apartment, but we never got to know them well.

My relationship with Will continued as if nothing had happened. We never discussed the abortion. I did notice after some time that Will got busier, was involved in multiple projects that required many more assistants. He was often unavailable due to conferences and classes he taught and begged out of our get-togethers, sometimes at the very last moment. Since I was also busy studying for exams, dealing with Jason and his complicated babysitting arrangements, and since Carlos was traveling to South America even more often than before, I did not think too much of it. Whenever we saw each other after he'd missed a meeting, Will was always loving and gentle and very apologetic. I had more time to spend with Jason and did not feel cheated.

It was never difficult for Will to find students who could take my place as his assistant when, due to babysitting problems, I could not attend to my professional responsibilities. Being Jason's mother was the most important job in the world, I firmly believed, and I was grateful that Will never argued about it and never appeared jealous of my time with Jason. Actually now that I think of it, he did not appear jealous of my time away from him at all. He was always ready to do something else, jump to another of his projects with Dave, or Len, or Abe. One student in particular, Scott Tessier, was always there ready to help, it seemed. When we were first introduced, I noticed a special closeness between Will and Scott. I remember thinking that Will was fortunate for having such good friends in his assistants. As time went by, I would occasionally become jealous of Dave, Len, and Abe. They were spending so much more time with Will. My time was fractured and partitioned by my obligations to Jason and my failing marriage. But such emotions were short lived.

Carlos seemed unaware of my absences as long as I had dinner ready when he was home and took care of Jason.

Taking care of Jason, after all, was my job, not his. He was my husband and Jason's father. He was supposed to provide for his family, but not waste his time with us. His job was more important. And so were numerous debates of Venezuelan or Chilean politics with his Latino friends.

As far as I remember, Carlos never actually talked to Jason or read him a book or kissed him before he went to bed. He rarely talked to me, except about mundane topics such as household chores or money issues. His salary was adequate for our immediate needs, but he was constantly preoccupied with money. After dinner, he would excuse himself from the table to make phone calls or read the papers. During weekends, he sometimes took care of the dry cleaning and shopped for food, but mostly he went out for drinks and to talk politics. The chores he did grudgingly, but since his frequent travels required clean shirts, it was easier for him to take them to the dry cleaners than wait for me to iron them.

His business in South America expanded and he was there more than in New York. And, of course, when he was there he spent time with his numerous relatives discussing Venezuelan politics ad nauseam. If we entertained at home, his friends, all of them Venezuelan or South American, would gather away from their wives and discuss politics and world economics, and soccer. Carlos argued in a booming voice, ignoring interruptions. He repeated his amusing stories of his many travels and basked in the laughter and praise, seeking to be the center of attention at all times. Infrequently I would plan dinners with my American friends, but those dinners were quieter, and Carlos more often than not found reasons to absent himself and leave me to entertain what he considered *my friends*. His nonappearance disappointed and frustrated me, even humiliated me in front of my friends, who seldom acknowledged equal disappointment or mentioned its oddness. Some considered Carlos eccentric and self-absorbed, but did not discuss his character with me in any detail, probably afraid to hurt my feelings.

When we entertained at home, Carlos was eager to show off his possessions, including his wife. He often brought items back from his travels and discussed their provenance in great detail. Although he strongly disapproved of my interest in journalism and film, seeing no great potential for earning power in such professions, he would often find ways to bring into conversation with our guests that I was in graduate school. The information seemed totally superfluous, because most of them already knew it.

He rarely complimented me on my looks, although once he made a big commotion about a dress I wore because it happened to be red. It was a nice red wool dress, originally expensive that I had bought on sale. I planned to wear it during Christmas holidays, since I considered the color of the dress particularly appropriate for the holiday season. An elderly Venezuelan couple, old friends of his parents on a short visit to New York, was coming to dinner, and I put on the red dress. Carlos made me change, because in his mind a red dress was too provocative. He did not wish to give the wrong impression to the friends of his parents. A few days later, Carlos returned the dress to the store since I refused to do it, partly because it no longer had the price tag and partly because I wanted to keep it. But Carlos managed to return it, despite the missing price tag and the fact that it had been on sale.

Will occasionally indicated that his academic pursuits

were temporary and that his real aspirations lay in making full-length features films in Hollywood. Such a move did not seem likely in the near future, and we seldom talked about it, preferring to discuss more immediate projects. When he did talk about movies, he would criticize the fake reality of Hollywood, its blindness to real issues, and proclaim that if he were in Hollywood, he would provide a more accurate mirror into human relationships. Uncertain about the precise nature of his future films, he vacillated among genres and techniques, plots, and themes. I could detect a desire to be socially relevant, concerned about human rights, but not restricted to an existing culture. At times he even seemed depressed.

"Everything has been said already," he said. "It is difficult to find your own voice."

"Follow your instinct; follow your emotions," I said, trying to be helpful. "Describe the contradictions within yourself."

"Yes, I would like to be provocative. Expose societal inconsistencies and portray stories in a larger context. Protest! I would like to force the audience to stretch their minds and be able to see a different reality. But the very setting we choose as the background for our internal tragedies is determined by our culture. We are products of cultural patterns within us. The culture is restrictive. I would like to overcome these restrictions."

Not be culturally determined? How did one achieve that? Suspended in air among different social domains, I could find no anchors. It was not a particularly comfortable way of life. I wanted to argue for culture-determined states, if for no other reason than to feel more secure, but there was a preponderance of evidence that culture-determined existence was a fantasy and did not exist permanently. If I were to explore this topic in more depth, I would have selected to examine how the cultural identity evolved and what exactly influenced its course of change.

All my efforts to get Will to describe any of his future endeavors in some detail were in vain. And if I persisted, he would change the subject. With the multitude of other subjects to talk about, it did not strike me as strange or prognostic of any deeply buried or hidden agendas. I was blindly in love. I was happy.

Four

As I entered the apartment, the first thing I saw was an array of shopping bags filled with Jason's toys. There was his favorite stuffed dog with floppy ears, the ears hanging over the edge of one of the shopping bags. In the evenings, I would sometimes tell Jason that we both needed some quiet time to read. I would open my textbooks to try to study, while Jason would drag over a heavy book on the history of philosophy and look at pictures of the philosophers, pretending to read. For some unexplained reason, this was his favorite book. And now it was prominently featured in one of the shopping bags, together with *Cat in the Hat, Green Eggs and Ham, Bartholomew and the Oobleck.* And there was Jason trying to stuff a toy in yet another shopping bag.

"What are you doing, Jason?"

"Packing."

"Are you packing your toys to take to Grandma's?"

"No! There are plenty of my toys at Grandma's. I don't need to take these toys there. These are my toys for here."

"So why are you packing them in shopping bags? Where are you going to take them?"

"You talked to Daddy on the phone yesterday and told him that it would be difficult to move to Caracas, because you don't have time to pack everything, because you have so much to do in school. I packed my toys so you won't have to. I wanted to help."

I sat down on the floor and embraced him, crying, immensely touched by his offer to help as ambivalent feelings crowded my heart and soul. Ambivalent feelings of guilt and yearning for a life in which my son did not have to pack toys, did not have to leave, and had a father who was not mostly absent. A father who took him to the zoo, taught him how to hold a baseball bat, or throw a football. A father whom I did not have to beg to come home when he promised and not several days later. A father who did not say he would give me a fur coat for my next birthday, but just bought me a paperback book and perhaps a rose and spent the rest of the night making love to me. I cried for the life I imagined with Will. A life with Will and Jason.

It was easy to decide to get a divorce, but Carlos was in Caracas. I did not want to discuss divorce over the phone. I felt I owed Carlos at least that much. I had to do it face to face, in person. So I had no choice. I had to go to Caracas, ask Carlos for divorce, and come back with Jason to complete my graduate work toward my PhD in journalism.

Carlos had been in Caracas for several months now. That he might remain there even longer was a distinct possibility. He often mentioned it but nothing was settled. Perhaps the next phone call ... The business opportunities were outstanding, he told me. He had been offered a big promotion as the head of the branch office in Caracas, with a substantial increase in salary. His family was there. His friends were there. He was looking forward to a boost in our social life and status.

Carlos assumed that all job-related decisions were his and that I, as his dutiful wife, would follow without objection or complaints. That my graduate studies would be interrupted was a minor issue, hardly worth a thought. Since we hadn't had the chance for a serious discussion about a permanent move to Caracas and what it would mean to my future professional life, and since no decisions had been made, I thought that this would be a good time to broach the topic of my staying in New York to finish my studies—and a divorce.

In the fall I asked for a semester's leave of absence from the university and made preparations for the move to Caracas. The apartment was rented and most of the furniture sold. I packed the rest with a heavy heart, full of misgivings. I explained to Will that the move was temporary and that as soon I told Carlos that I wanted a divorce, I would be back in New York with Jason.

Will accepted my reasons and expressed only minimal reservations about my decision to go to Caracas. Anxious and confused, I was so ambivalent about the trip, I made no specific plans for the future. I just hoped I could stay with my parents when Jason and I returned to New York. There was this expectation, poorly formed, illusory, about my future life with Will. Will and I talked about living together constantly, but made no realistic plans. In my wildest dreams, I could not foresee how costly those illusions would prove to be. At the time I fervently wished that all of this would be over or that I did not have to do or think about any of it. That life would sort itself out without my intervention.

Jason was less ambivalent. He was genuinely looking forward to his next trip by plane, meeting new friends, and learning to speak Spanish better. He could already understand a lot and was proud that he could count to a hundred in Spanish. Someone had given him a puzzle about the geography of Venezuela and he often played with it, pleased that he could show off his knowledge of his father's native land. Puzzles were among his favorite toys.

My first impressions of Caracas were mixed. It was hot and humid and people on the crowded streets were loud, always jostling one another, always shouting. The traffic was unbearably noisy, decibels above the comfort level, traffic lights sporadic, traffic rules unclear. There were few traffic signs and I got easily lost. People drove with their left arms extended out their car windows, signaling when making turns because most car lights were out of order and nobody paid any attention to them. None of the cars had air-conditioning, despite the heat and humidity.

Caracas was not an ideal place to learn to drive, but that is where I learned. On my second lesson, the driving instructor took me to a busy intersection in the center of the city, into the middle of the traffic pandemonium. Not seeing any clear signs on how to proceed and which avenue to turn into, I asked, bewildered, "Who goes first?"

"The driver! The person at the wheel!" he said. "You are driving, aren't you? Don't be afraid. Look around at all the other idiots driving."

Well, I thought, if it was up to me, since I was the driver, I'd better do it fast, before someone else cut me off. Thrusting my left arm out the open car window to signal that I intended to turn left, I successfully completed the turn into the correct lane of the avenue and in the right direction. The driving instructor said nothing, but I was sure I detected a brief smile.

The street on which we lived was relatively quiet. The tall apartment building was walled off from the street to provide additional privacy, and bougainvillea flowers were everywhere, cheerfully overflowing the walls with vivid pink, red, and purple blossoms. The rented apartment was furnished and far more spacious than I expected. There was a large living room with sliding doors to the terrace, three bedrooms, two bathrooms, a kitchen with servants' quarters next to it, which included yet another bedroom and a separate bathroom.

The biggest change in our standard of living was to have a maid. Her name was Raquel. I was delighted and at the same time very naïve. At first I wanted to be friends with her and left it up to her to do what she thought needed to be done. Luckily she had lots of experience working with other American families and was used to this rather unorthodox arrangement. I taught her how to prepare dishes that Carlos liked; she introduced me to Venezuelan dishes and made absolutely delicious *arepas* for breakfast for Jason.

Several American families lived in the same building. Jason started the first grade and made instant friends with two girls from one of those families. They all went to an international school with instruction in English. Most kids in the school were Venezuelan, and Jason was quickly learning more Spanish as well. At first my Spanish was bookish. I had taken classes in Spanish grammar in New York in order to be able to speak correctly and grammatically to my husband's family and friends. Jason's Spanish was more immediate and more useful, the everyday kind. He became indispensable as my interpreter with Raquel.

I don't know whether Raquel noticed how distracted and depressed I was. Perhaps she attributed my anxiety to not knowing Spanish and not being able to explain clearly what I expected her to do. Since my stilted Spanish was probably overly formal and inadequate in the beginning, Carlos often gave her daily instructions. He also paid her. She was much more at ease with him in charge than with me. Their conversations seemed friendly, sprinkled with teasing and laughter. With me Raquel was polite but short.

After about a month in Caracas I started having heavy periods and consulted my American friends about a gynecologist. They recommended Lydia. Many of her patients were American. She shared an office with another doctor, a pediatrician. There was no receptionist, and the large waiting room was crowded with mothers with children of various ages. The older children played with one another while the younger children played with toys strewn on the floor. The mothers talked to one another, some holding smaller children in their laps. The pediatrician was a man in his sixties, white haired and somewhat disheveled, but his demeanor was friendly. In a booming voice he would greet the mother of the next patient as he motioned them into his office. Each mother was treated as if she were his long-lost relative that he was overjoyed to see again.

"*¡Señora Sanchez—Maria Elena, que gusto de verte, mi hijita! ¿Y don Manuelito como estas? ¡No llores mi hijito! ¿Y porque sigues llorando? ¡Como te estas cresido! ¡De veras te pareces a tu papa! ¿No es cierto, Maria Elena?*

¡Casi un hombre ya! Voy contigo enseguida—pero primero tengo que ver al bébé, Joaquin, que vino con su abuelita, Martha."

"*¿Martha, que tal? ¿Como sigue Enrique en su nuevo trabajo? ¿Y la casa? ¿Ya terminaron con el jardin? ¿Van a poner una piscina para que Joaquin aprenda a nadar?*"

The mothers with babies and smaller children were taken in before older children, out of turn. This made perfect sense to me and it subdued the clamor remarkably. The nurse seemed to know every child and greeted them by their names, chatting pleasantly with their mothers, asking about mutual friends, offering advice, and commiserating about sad news.

When I entered the waiting room hesitantly and alone, the nurse knew immediately that I was there to see the other doctor. She announced my presence to Lydia. I did not have to wait at all, because apparently all of the waiting patients were there to see the pediatrician.

Lydia had dark hair in an elegant upswept hairdo, a few escaped strands caressing her cheeks. She wore make-up that made her dark eyes even more expressive and vivid red lipstick. Under her starched white coat, her clothes were fashionable and obviously expensive, although the effect was pleasing, reassuring, giving her an air of quality and competent confidence. At first she addressed me in excellent English, almost devoid of any accent, but soon switched to Spanish when I indicated I understood what she was saying. In Spanish she addressed me as *tu* rather than *usted,* and mixed a chummy sisterly Spanish with more quietly professional English.

The visit resulted in lots of worries. In a few days, Lydia called me to tell me that my Pap smear was positive.

I knew what that meant. Lydia suggested I have immediate treatment, the loop electrosurgical excision procedure, or LEEP, as a first step. The procedure could be done in her office and usually required only local anesthesia. She wanted to schedule it for my next visit. I trusted Lydia and her judgment, but postponed the decision.

Lydia was the only woman in her class to finish medical school. Two other women who started with her did not graduate. From a wealthy family, she and her younger sister and two older brothers were educated abroad, in Paris and the States. Her late father had been a well-known cardiologist in Caracas with a huge practice. Her sister did not pursue a professional career. Her two brothers were dentists and had a joint practice. Lydia completed her OB-GYN residency at Johns Hopkins Hospital. When she returned to Caracas she became one of the four women gynecologists in Venezuela. She was married and had four children. But of course, she also had two nannies, a maid, and a woman who came weekly to do the laundry.

Carlos and I were invited to her home for dinner, and Lydia's brother-in-law gave me the third degree about my professional life.

"Do you have children?" he asked.

"Yes, I have a son. He just started first grade."

"We have six," he said proudly.

"Your wife must have full hands!"

"Yes, she does, but luckily she has no aspirations to work outside, unlike her sister Lydia."

I did not like to hear Lydia's motherhood diminished by her courage to have a profession. "I am a professional myself," I said. "I am not sure I would like to stay home just to take care of my children, even if I had six children."

"But Carlos said you are at home. A professional? A professional is someone with a responsible position, a title, a graduate degree, a member of a professional society." He spoke with an air of superiority, certain that I had none of these.

"I am an ABD in journalism and film," I said.

"An ABD? What's on earth is an ABD?" he asked, sounding incredulous.

"An ABD is a person who finished the course work for a PhD, collected data for a dissertation, and has not finished writing the thesis. It means, 'all but the dissertation.'"

"I have to tell Carlos to make you pregnant immediately, so you will forget about this dissertation of yours." He laughed heartily at his comment. I did not.

The coffee was served in another room, where I found myself surrounded by wives and mothers. Although I could hear a loud discussion of Venezuelan politics from the other room, Carlos being the loudest, the ladies discussed children and hairdos and soap operas. Lydia, completely at ease, joined in with a story about her nanny, Viviana, who insisted that Juanito, Lydia's youngest son, brush his teeth every time after saying *mierda*.

When I learned about my positive Pap smear, I wished for a pair of strong hands, Will's hands, around me and his whisper in my ear that all would be fine. I wanted my father's advice, and begged Carlos to go to New York for a second opinion. Carlos agreed. The doctor I saw in New York said to wait six months and repeat the Pap smear. He was of the old school and despised aggressive treatments of any kind, advocating expectant medical management. I did not see Will. He was in California. I went back to Caracas. Lydia again insisted I have the LEEP. I decided to wait.

In the meantime, Will wrote me letters in which he said he was impatient to go to California, to Hollywood, and make a real film, a feature film. He wanted to know when I was going to tell Carlos that I wanted a divorce. He wanted to know how large an apartment to look for, or maybe a house and a dog for Jason in California. I kept postponing my confrontation with Carlos for a "more propitious time," not realizing that the more Jason felt at home in Caracas, the more difficult all this would be.

With my positive Pap smear scare, I deliberated even longer, wishing it all to go away. Carlos and I had no sex life. He was content with his demanding job and frequent visits with his extended family, where he could engage in long and passionate arguments about recent developments in Venezuelan public life. I made friends among the other American families in the building and through members of Carlos's extended family.

It was a couple of weeks before Christmas. I had not heard from Will for a while. The last letter had been about a month earlier. Given the frequency of his letters before, this was unusual. Caracas did not have well-organized mail delivery. It was no doubt complicated with houses and buildings not having numbers. The streets had names, usually for some important person, as did sectors of the city. We lived in La Florida, on the Avenida Las Acacias, in the building called La Americana.

La Americana had rows of tiny mailboxes on the first floor, each illegibly labeled with what I surmised were family names. That was where I collected Will's letters, all addressed to me, but with various, often hilarious made-up senders. Our other mail, including the personal mail from my parents, my sister, and my friends, and all the magazines and packages, were sent to Carlos's office, which he considered much safer.

I did not realize that the postmen in Caracas had a habit of collecting the mail a few weeks before Christmas and then delivering it all at once to the *ama de casa* for the Christmas *propina*. That is, the tip, which was usually substantial, given for their hard work over the year. Since most American families living in La Americana did not get any mail, the postman felt shortchanged in terms of his Christmas *propina*. He was delighted with Will's prolific output and happily delivered some twenty letters to Raquel, who just as happily gave them to Carlos in turn for substantial monetary reward for both of them. Needless to say, Raquel ceased to be my friend at that point, and I was in big trouble. However, I did not learn about this until several weeks after Christmas. All I knew at first was that Will's letters were no more.

Carlos's comportment changed. He demanded a detailed schedule of my every day, what I was planning to do, where I was planning to go, and who I would see. If I said I was planning to meet a friend, he would demand to know when, where, and for how long.

He would suddenly appear at the hairdresser's to take me home with the excuse that during that time of day it was difficult to get a taxi. When I tried to explain that I planned to walk the ten or twelve blocks, he would come up with dubious stories of street crime in Caracas and how it was unsafe to walk. When I protested that in the part of Caracas where we lived, street crime was unheard of, he said he had read about it in the papers just the other day. He asked for exhaustive lists for food shopping and the names of the stores where I planned to do it. He called several times during the day and asked to talk to Raquel, saying he had instructions for changes in dinner menus; and even appeared in person, saying he had forgotten items that were needed that very moment.

Our bedroom closets were separated, with my clothes on the right side and his suits on the left side. Suddenly he kept organizing my clothes, emptying the drawers and throwing my underwear on the bed; putting things back in a different order so that I sometimes could not find the articles I wanted. When I caught him rummaging through my jewelry box, he said he was looking for his gold cufflinks, although he seldom wore shirts that required cufflinks. He was forever rearranging books on the shelves in the spare room—we called the library—and searched for real or imaginary lost items under the sofa.

If I mentioned having seen a friend, he would ask what we talked about and then make cynical remarks about our friendship. He would say that one could not trust friends these days and that everybody had ulterior motives. He would sullenly criticize what he read in papers or saw on TV, and would often get up in the middle of a news program to do something else. We stopped seeing friends, and our socializing became limited to his family members. The excuse was that friends were untrustworthy and it was family that counted. He tried to arrange my social calendar so that I spent time with various members of his family. I felt chaperoned, supervised, and bored. Two of his female cousins who were older than I and had several children did not work and had never gone to college. Their immediate concerns revolved around clothing, hairdos, children, meals, and their unreliable household help. During visits with these cousins I was forced to speak Spanish, but I did not enrich my vocabulary or endear myself to these people, since I tried in vain to change the topic of conversation to current events, educational aspirations for their children, or new trends in films. Their film interests were limited to the plights and tribulations of the characters in Mexican soap operas or the marriages and divorces of the actors playing in them. The superficiality and boredom always made me smoke more than I intended, and these social occasions always ended with a fierce headache.

Jason's close friend from school, Reid, came over occasionally to play with Jason. They built cardboard houses and roads for their Matchbox cars, did puzzles, and watched TV, later enacting Superman tales for my amusement. Reid was usually fetched by his mother, who had another baby at home and lived close by. She was a slightly overweight jolly woman from Edinburgh, who spoke with a pronounced Scottish accent. Although I enjoyed her company, she rarely had time to stay and chat because even with a maid, she was always in hurry to bathe the baby, or go to the market, or make supper. She made me laugh with the stories of her harried life as the mother of a newborn who was forever hungry, or had just soiled her diaper after a bath and a complete change of clothes, and who outgrew her dresses in days. She never criticized anything and was forever cheerful. Her blonde hair was always a little disheveled and her shorts and blouses wrinkled. Once when her shirt had a bright orange stain of the carrots her baby had just vomited, she nonchalantly apologized for not having the time to change and laughed it off. She did not like Carlos and resisted all my efforts to get our families to socialize.

One evening before Christmas, while Reid and Jason

were watching TV, the doorbell sounded. When I opened the door, there was Reid's father full of apology for not coming sooner to fetch Reid. I invited him in and called Reid, but Reid begged his father to stay a little longer until the program they were watching was finished. Reid's father smiled indulgently and saw nothing wrong with granting his son this rare privilege. The program would be finished in about fifteen minutes.

"Come sit down," I said, gesturing to the living room. "Would you like to have a drink?"

"I would not mind a drink. Scotch without ice, if you have it.'

"But of course." I poured him a finger's worth of Chivas as taught by Carlos.

Reid's father took the crystal glass from me and sat down on the sofa, obviously in good mood.

"Our kids have jolly good time, eh?" He smiled and sipped his drink. "When I was Reid's age I spent much more time outside with my friends. But Scotland is so much colder than Caracas. It is an adjustment to live here."

"It is. It is," I agreed. "No snow for Christmas. It will be our first Christmas in the summer."

"This year we aren't going to Scotland for the holiday. The baby's just too small for travel. I guess Reid misses the snow too. When I was his age, we once had a pissing contest in the snow to see who could piss farther. And I won! Must have been all the tea I drank before."

We both laughed at the image of our kids having a pissing contest in the snow. At that moment Carlos opened the door and saw us drinking Scotch—well, saw Reid's father drinking Scotch from his favorite crystal glass, the bottle of Chivas on the table—and both of us laughing loudly, enjoying each other's company. He was not amused.

"What do you think you are doing?" he aggressively demanded of Reid's father.

Obviously taken aback by Carlos's belligerence, Reid's father stood up. He was only about five foot ten, so Carlos towered over him.

"Nothing," he said to Carlos. "I was just waiting for Reid, for the TV program to end ..."

Reid emerged from Jason's room, smiling, but was soon bewildered by his father's apologetic demeanor.

Taking hold of Reid's shoulder, Carlos rudely pushed him toward the door. Reid's father still stood by the sofa, and Carlos shouted at him, "I don't want you or your son ever again in my house. Do you hear? Never again. Is that clear?"

Both Reid and his father almost ran toward the elevator, shouting, "Okay, okay. Fine. We are leaving."

When the elevator doors closed behind them, Carlos walked to the kitchen, yelling for Raquel to serve dinner. I tried to stop him.

"What is the matter with you? Why were you so rude?"

Carlos pushed me away and sat at the dinner table. "Let's just eat. I'll deal with you later."

"Dad, what happened? Did Reid do something? Did he do that?"

He pointed at the crystal glass, which was on the floor, the Scotch sinking into the carpet. Reid's father must have overturned it in his rush to leave.

"I'm sure he didn't mean to do it, Dad," Jason said as he picked up the glass and put it on the coffee table.

"Wash your hands and come to the dinner table, Jason," Carlos said. "You hear me?"

Jason obediently went to wash his hands. When he appeared at the dinner table, he looked downcast, huge question marks fluttering on his lashes, and quietly sat down. I had made dinner earlier, Jason's favorite meal, breaded veal cutlets and spinach. Raquel just had to serve it, but Carlos made a production of thanking Raquel for her effort, ignoring the scene that just happened.

Reid never came back to play with Jason. I had no explanation for Carlos's rude behavior.

"Alexandra, what did Reid do at your home?" Reid's mother asked on the phone the next day. "Carlos was so upset with him."

I could not tell her that Carlos was not upset with Reid, since I suspected he was upset with me.

Days went by, and all my trips to the mailbox on the first floor left me empty handed. There were no more letters from Will. With Christmas approaching and my parents' anticipated visit, I was too busy to dwell on why there were no letters. I assumed Will had gone on vacation for the holidays. I also still did not find an opportune moment to mention divorce to Carlos. I hoped my parents' visit would provide me with an opportunity, perhaps, to discuss my future life and how I would support myself in case this proved an issue for the custody of Jason. I never doubted Jason would be living with me.

That Christmas in Caracas was our first Christmas without snow. It was very festive and very different from the States. The streets were decorated with dazzling images of red, yellow, orange, and green flowers, butterflies, and birds; there was not a Santa Claus in sight. The splendor of all of this vibrant and intense color transformed the city into a lavish and cheerful fairy tale. The festivities were influenced by the predominantly Catholic religious customs and started on the sixteenth of December with a daily mass, ending with the midnight mass on the twenty-fourth, *Misa de Gallo*. Traditionally the festivities lasted until the sixth of January, *Dia de los Reyes Magos*. In the evenings groups of people gathered with their instruments and sang Christmas carols in intriguing contrapuntal harmony, called *aguinaldos*, accompanied by *cuatros, flautas, maracas*, and *el furruco*, the drum. Everybody was cheerful and happy.

There were many parties whose tone was frivolous and optimistic, with loud music, lots of special holiday dishes, and presents for children. Many people got drunk and danced until dawn. It was all very enjoyable and friendly.

Jason loved his presents and was happy to see his grandparents. My father gave him a chess set. Jason fell in love with the game, and they played for hours. Carlos, as was his custom, announced what he wanted for Christmas months in advance and was happy that he got most of the items on his list. Since Raquel was given days off, I cooked and my mother baked her favorite nut cake. I even tried making *hallacas*, the traditional Venezuelan Christmas dish with cornmeal and palm leaves. The result was a disaster and I vowed not to do it again. Not, at least, until Raquel was back to supervise the process. The other dishes, *pan de hamon* with raisins and olives and *dulce de lechosa*, were given to us by some friendly neighbors. The American families in the building exchanged homemade cookies. It was customary to have at least seven different kinds.

My parents left soon after the New Year. Carlos, who

was back to normal during the holidays, assumed his gloomy demeanor as soon as my parents were gone. And the stormy clouds broke into a diluvium. Carlos confronted me with Will's letters that he had collected before Christmas. Most of the envelopes had been torn open in haste. Some appeared to be Xeroxed copies. Carlos furiously demanded explanations. His voice alternated between loud, angry shrieking and sputtering hissing. The sound was irritating, piercing the after-holiday quiet, disturbing the humidity entering through the open terrace doors. I remember sitting without words in a gray wingchair, immobile in the sudden onslaught of his anger and trying in vain to protect myself from this inevitable confrontation. As he described how he got the letters and learned of my immense betrayal, I felt without recourse, drowning in the vast regret and sorrow that I had not told him sooner.

"Who is Will?"

"Did you sleep with him?"

"How long have you known him?"

"Do you love him?"

A barrage of unending questions that I didn't know how to answer, each question, a new assault. All the questions were repeated again and again. I finally spoke.

"Carlos, I want a divorce."

"You want a divorce? You want a ... divorce? You are never getting a divorce. I am a good husband. I gave you a good home. I am a good provider. You have no reason to ask for divorce."

"I love him."

"What about me?"

"I don't love you anymore, Carlos," I whispered.

"Well, we will see about that. You are not to write to

him again, you hear? You are not to contact him again, you hear? I am going to stop all this."

"Carlos, I want a divorce."

"I don't care what you want. You are *not* getting a divorce. *Not* getting a divorce."

The accusations continued into the night. The dark outside was getting lighter as morning approached. We were both exhausted. Carlos looked at his watch.

"I am taking a shower and going to work. You will stay here and will not see anyone or talk to anyone, you hear?"

Jason woke up and I helped him get dressed, eat breakfast, and go to school. Then went to bed and slept until he came home in the afternoon. I woke up in a daze, defeated by circumstances, unable to think clearly, yearning for Will's assurances that everything would be all right again. But they would not.

Once Carlos learned about my infidelities through the confiscated letters, he was not sure whether he had the whole story and started interrogating me about details. He would come home from work in a foul mood; we would eat dinner in silence or talk about mundane things if Jason was present or when we had guests; and then after dinner the interrogations started. He kept repeating the same questions over and over, while I sat in the same gray chair with my legs folded under. I came to hate that wingchair. Every time I happened to look at it during the day, I was filled with incipient dread of the after-dinner interrogations.

"When did the affair start?"

"Do you love him?"

"Does our marriage mean nothing to you?"

"Does Jason know that you are a whore?"

"I am not a whore. I fell in love with Will. I don't know when it started exactly. I was lonely. You traveled and left me alone."

"I traveled? I had to earn the money to feed us all! How do you think I could do that without traveling?"

"When you came home, you never had time for Jason and me. You were always out with friends."

"I was not always out with friends. I called from Caracas every day."

"No, you did not! Maybe once a week. I never knew when you'd be back."

"That was to your advantage so you could spend the time with your lover? Where did he take you? Did Jason go with you?"

"He took Jason to the zoo. You never did!" I managed to sound accusatory.

"I never did? I had to work and make sure we had money to live."

"Your salary is not bad, and my parents always helped."

"Your parents? Did your mother babysit when you were with your lover?"

"It's enough, Carlos. I am tired. I want to go to bed."

"Not yet. I need to know more. I want the details on how you cheated."

"Carlos, I do not love you anymore. I want a divorce. Let me go."

"Let you go? You want a divorce?"

"Yes, I want a divorce."

He was silent and then spoke as if he'd thought of something. "Okay. You can go, but Jason stays."

"You cannot care for Jason while you work. Jason belongs with me."

"So your lover can be his father?" And then, vehemently, louder, "Not as long as I live!"

After another pause he declared, "You are not going anywhere. Jason is not going anywhere. There will be no more love letters. I will make sure that you do not see him again, hear him again, communicate with him ever again. You hear?" He was shouting now. "You hear?"

Very loud. So loud that I heard Jason come out from his room in his pajamas, sleepy and almost crying,

"What is going on? Daddy, why are you shouting? Mommy, why are you crying?"

"It's nothing, Jason, darling. I love you. Go back to bed."

Jason would not go alone. Relieved that I could escape further verbal assaults, cross-examination and the torrent of questions, I got out of the gray chair, hugged him, and took him back to bed. Thankfully Carlos did not interfere with that and I was grateful to be able to end the daily quota of reproach. But the next day it started again: the same questions, same threats, same shouting, identical rebuke.

I am not sure how much Jason understood. During the days I kept my thoughts and feelings concealed and buried. In Jason's presence, it was not too difficult to be in a good mood. He was imaginative in his games, curious about everything, and I delighted in answering his constant questions. He told me about his days in school, about his friends and what they talked about. I could tell he was learning fast. In his conversations with Raquel it was obvious his Spanish was excellent and almost without an accent. With me, he spoke English. He proudly read to me in English. He would stop at a word he did not understand, impatient, until I said it and explained its meaning. We made up stories. Before going to bed we would read together and talk. Carlos never once read to him or spent much time with him. During dinner, his conversations were short and he bided his time until Jason was in bed and I returned to the living room, to start with the torture—I his captive in the gray wingchair.

This went on for weeks. I was exhausted and depressed. After Jason left for school in the morning and Carlos to work, I returned to bed weak and shattered. I felt betrayed by life, by love, and had no strength to fight back and reclaim hope. The heat and humidity of Caracas, which seemed tolerable at first, now became oppressive, and sometimes I could hardly breathe. The apartment had no air conditioning. As was the custom in Caracas, there were no proper windows, just glass or wooden slats kept permanently open. The bright colors of bougainvillea now served as a reminder of happier days and made me even more miserable. It seemed my life had changed into a shadowy existence without any right to colors and brightness. I was so very tired and slept a lot. Upon waking I did not feel rested at all and went through motions of everyday chores by rote. Every decision was difficult. Every action seemed beyond my strength. Brushing my teeth in the morning seemed unnecessary and taking a shower required a major decision.

When Jason was home, I felt an obligation to be less unhappy. I feared that I had lost my identity as a person, as a sexual being, so the only identity left was the one of mother to Jason. I clung to it fiercely, determined not to lose this vestige of me, wishing to be the best mother I could, grasping at motherhood, hanging on to the last shreds, last remnants of identity.

Carlos went to New York to confront Will, but I never learned what exactly happened. After their meeting I received several letters from Will, but they left me utterly confused. In the first letter, mailed to Carlos' office address, he told me that our affair was over and our relationship had no future; that Carlos loved me and wished for a second chance, which we should give him; that he was going to California to make full-length movies and was no longer interested in academic work. He urged me to forget him and to resurrect my original feelings for Carlos. I could not believe what I read and was enormously hurt. The ache was physical, affecting my entire body. I could not breathe. I felt crushed. I reread the letter again and again. No, it was not possible! This was not Will talking. We had known each other for a short time, but intensely and deeply. How could he forget our intense, passionate, and powerful relationship so quickly, so thoroughly? Where had he found the strength to cut me out of his life? Where had he learned this unfamiliar skill of a surgeon with a scalpel? I felt betrayed, angry, and alone.

How did these two men claim the right to decide my destiny? Why was I not consulted? Why did I not count? Feeling powerless and impotent, I cried. I slept, and when awake, I cried. The tears kept hurtling down my cheeks. I could not stop them no matter what thoughts entered my mind. I tried distracting myself with television and reading, but could not concentrate on anything. It lasted for days.

After several months, taking a chance, I looked and found another letter in the mailbox at home, close to my birthday. This time Will wrote that he still loved me and that we should be optimistic about our future. He urged me again to try to get a divorce. I was confused and conflicted, but suddenly hopeful. The heat and humidity of Caracas felt less oppressive. The blue sky seemed full of possibility. All hope requires a bit of blindness. The bougainvillea got back its color, and I thought I heard birds chirping. I had my hair cut and styled, put on lipstick and a dress that had languished in the closet for months unworn. And I found courage to talk to Carlos about divorce again. He would not hear about it.

I borrowed money from some American friends and bought two tickets to New York for myself and Jason and started searching for our passports. There were not in the usual place. I searched for them in all the possible places and finally had to ask Carlos.

"Why do you need passports?" he asked.

"I bought airline tickets to New York. My father is sick and I want to visit my parents."

This was only partly a subterfuge. My father had been diagnosed with cancer and I really wanted to see my parents. I felt abysmally alone and needed them—even my sister, whom I had not been very close with during the years of my marriage. But Carlos just laughed.

"You wasted your money! By the way, where did you get the money for tickets?"

I was silent.

"You are not going anyplace."

He waited, but I said nothing. He laughed derisively again. "Actually, if you want to go to New York, be my guest, go. But Jason stays here."

"I do not want to leave Jason here. I have a ticket for Jason. Jason is going with me."

"Jason stays here. Jason is not going anyplace. Jason is my son."

"Jason is my son too. My parents would love to see him."

"You think I don't know what you are planning?"

"I am not planning anything. I just want to visit my parents."

"And not come back? Maybe go to California to look for your boyfriend? I don't think he wants you there."

It seemed hopeless. Carlos would not release the passports and my tickets expired.

Carlos was suspicious of all of my friends and would not let me see them. I could only socialize with his relatives; his two cousins became my constant companions. I smoked a lot and felt cut off from any joy or pleasure.

When I managed to go anyplace alone, I kept seeing Will's countenance in every face around me. Once or twice I followed bearded men, convinced they were Will, hoping he had come to take me with him. I dreamed of him constantly, but in each dream he went away without saying good-bye and his image receded, until it was lost in ambiguous points of departure.

I continued to sleep away half the day, getting up more tired than before. I spent hours in the gray wingchair, thinking of nothing in particular. When I tried to concentrate, I could not hold a thought in my mind. Out on the terrace, I contemplated sailing out into space, until reaching the parking lot below, twelve stories down ... Thoughts of suicide were relentless. I stopped changing clothes, never brushed my teeth, never combed my hair, which was growing longer and thinner. My clothes did not fit me well, but my appearance stopped being of concern. I avoided looking in the mirror, because my reflection depressed me further.

At times I cooked a meal, but mostly I let Raquel decide on the menu and do the shopping for food. She ignored me and yet seemed to be in the same room whenever I answered the phone, as if to make sure I did not make unauthorized calls. I am sure she reported my whereabouts to Carlos in the most boring detail. I felt imprisoned. The only things I kept up with concerned Jason. I made sure I was there to wake him up and when he came home from school. I completed puzzles with him, played cards with him, sometimes watched television with him, and read him bedtime stories every evening. Dinners were mostly silent or passed in forced dialogues. The topics were less than ordinary, their purpose only to keep Jason from asking probing questions about my lack of energy and enthusiasm.

From my friends I learned that divorces were difficult in Venezuela, and that fathers had the right to custody of their male offspring until they were seven years old. Jason was too young yet to hope for a more positive outcome. I could try to survive until Jason was older. I also learned that Carlos was seeing a prominent lawyer who had suddenly became his best friend. This lawyer was very rich and traveled in his private jet. His wife was the daughter of a former well-known government official. They had ten children and were devout Catholics.

I went to see Lydia, hoping to get advice. But once in her office, I lost courage to talk about personal problems. She was busy. She assumed I came for medical reasons and she examined me. My Pap smear was again positive. Lydia was concerned. She diagnosed carcinoma in situ and urged me to have a hysterectomy. In my depressed state, I did not think too much about it. It seemed just one more of destiny's dirty tricks. There was nothing good in store for me in the future. The date was set, the surgery done. The recovery was relatively uneventful. The final result—no more children.

During all this time there were no more letters from Will. I heard from my sister that he'd resigned his teaching position in New York and gone to California. To Hollywood, I assumed.

The sadness bored deep into me and transformed me into a creature of hate, immobile in thought and action, a stranger. The nights I spent sunk deep in the pit of my disappointment, surrounded by the sharp icicles of Will's rejection, which penetrated the air and grew slowly toward me, touching my skin, spreading the coldness, stiffness, inability to move. In the mornings, I blew into my frozen palms some semblance of life and crawled painfully out of the abyss. I walked to Jason's room to wake him up, help him select what to wear, tie his shoes, comb his hair, and watch him eat breakfast that Raquel prepared.

"*¿Jason, que quieres hoy para el desayuno?*"

"*¡Arepitas!*"

"*¿Arepitas? Otra vez?*"

"*¡Si, si, si!*"

"*Pero las comiste ayer. ¿Hoy de nuevo?*"

"*Si, si si, Raquel. Sabes que me gustan. ¡Las quiero todos los dias!*"

"*¿Y no te aburres, mi niño?*"

Saved by Jason each morning. Kept sane by Jason. Kept

alive by Jason during each day and falling into the abyss of despair for having lost Will, having lost hope of having his love and hope for a normal life. I started wondering whose body Will was admiring now, sculpting a new Venus or a David?

I looked at my face and hair. Eyes red, bloodshot from crying, hair without bounce and little curl, flat, dark, unwashed. Looking at myself naked, I despaired even more. There was nothing beautiful about the body in the mirror: skinny, flat chested, bones sticking out on my hips, too-long legs, no waist, square hips. How could I think that Will, the handsome, attractive, exuberant Will, blue-eyed Will, could love this creature? Or was it that he did not love the woman in me that he'd awakened with his sensuality, but— Oh, God! The boy in me, the boyishness of my body. Was that what had attracted him?

I doubted everything. That realization joined the despair, insinuated itself into my mind. Full of uncertainties about my femininity, I sensed I was falling over the familiar precipice, falling, falling, pushing myself deeper into despair and the doubts about my femininity, his heterosexuality. I doubted his love, his intentions of taking me with him to California. Did he even exist? Did I make him up? Who was I? Who had I become? A desirable woman no longer, an unsuccessful journalist, a wife who cheated, trapped in a failed marriage. Was my role as a mother in jeopardy as well? My identity crumbled, lost; seemingly irretrievable.

Life stopped. Years went by, reflected only in Jason's face that kept changing as he grew. His eyes used to be wide with wonder and curiosity when he was small, absorbing everything around him with glee. The curiosity remained as he got older, but his questions became more specific. He listened to my explanations, always eager for more information. Often he incorporated what he was learning into his imagination. His room was transformed into wondrous landscapes, and he spent hours building and rebuilding his surroundings. One day the unknown, imagined landscape of Mars; at other times the familiar surroundings of the garden around our building, or the streets of New York. He raced cars noisily through it all and was reluctant to pick up the day's wonders before going to bed. The next day a new landscape would emerge.

Lydia recognized my despair but asked no questions. Through some friends from medical school, she got me a job at a research lab at the university. The topic of investigation was the role of infection in premature labor, its immunology in sheep. The head of the laboratory was an extroverted Swede, a physician interested in clinical research, who told me half in jest that I reminded him of a pagan goddess of spring and fertility and hired me on the spot. He was more often found on the tennis court than in the lab, but he was respected by his staff, which included several clinicians, OB-GYN specialists, an anatomist, an electron microscopist, a biochemist, a neurologist, several technicians, two clerks, and a secretary. When he was present everyone spoke English, but since I was to join the technicians, who spoke Spanish, I got to speak both languages interchangeably.

The lab occupied several floors, had its own electron microscope, and an extensive library. In the beginning, I was assistant to a Japanese gynecologic surgeon who spent an inordinate number of hours in the lab and clearly preferred lab work and research to clinical practice. His English was accented but precise. My first assignment was to correct his English in a manuscript based on some recent immunological studies, involving papilloma virus infection. I had a feeling I was reading Japanese, although it was written in English. After such a hiatus from anything academic, I threw myself into the work and soon presented him with an edited text of his manuscript. It at least sounded less Japanese and almost English. He seemed delighted with my work and my work ethics and gave me several of his already published articles to read to familiarize myself with his prior investigations.

The head of the lab instituted regular weekly meetings at which he often appeared asleep and would occasionally wake up to swat a fly with a newspaper, but this behavior was deceptive. He heard every word of every disposition. His comments, when he deemed them necessary, cut through the narratives of the Spanish-speaking staff with diamond precision, and he brought the meetings to a close with clear goals for the next week's work. I marveled at his genius and his talent and wished for an opportunity to show that I appreciated his guidance and scientific acumen.

I developed an easy working relationship with the Japanese surgeon. We collaborated on several studies and published papers, and that eventually granted me a MA and a PhD in reproductive physiology. He was an understanding advisor, fascinated with his work in immunology, a butterfly collector, and a friendly coworker. During our lunches, if there were others present, he would stubbornly maintain that Japanese men were intellectually superior to Japanese women and were never found in the kitchen or did any household chores. That all resonated well with the Venezuelans. When we were alone he urged me to read Yasunari Kawabata, and he would ask me with tears in his eyes whether I liked Kawabata's descriptions of Kyoto. He would whisper in secret how tired he was some mornings, because the night before they'd had company for dinner and he'd helped his wife tidy up and wash the dishes.

He frequently went into the jungle, loaded with overripe bananas, to collect butterflies, and would proudly show us the collected objects, describing their wing coloring and pointing at the differences from specimen to specimen. Some of the butterflies were huge, almost as big as moths. He never tired of showing the collections to anyone who wanted to see them. Some technicians would tease him about cruelty to animals and he would become genuinely angry, explaining that he was very considerate and respectful of nature.

He was tolerant with me when our experiments did not succeed, patiently advising me to read more, giving me articles and initiating analyses of our results in light of other findings. As we carried out studies designed to investigate viral infections as causes of preterm labor in pregnant ewes, I was glad that lamb was not often on the menu in Venezuelan restaurants.

The part of the university that housed our laboratory was on a hillside outside of Caracas, and the ride in the bus took more than forty minutes. I was glad to be working, although sometimes the hours away from home made me feel guilty for not spending more time with Jason. He was growing rapidly, changing rapidly from a little boy to an active and inquisitive young person.

Slowly, gradually, and with enormous effort, I unfolded from Will's rejection and his silence. It was not an easy road, burdened as I was under the weight of assorted grievances. Each step hurt as if my shoes were permanently filled with sharp-edged pebbles I could not shake off. The work in the lab helped dull the ragged edges of the loss at times more, at other times less successfully. An alien stillness enveloped my existence, raw and bleeding at times and never peaceful. I got used to living in perpetual transition. I counted good days on my fingers and tried to lose the count of bad days. But there were still many bad days, triple the amount of good days.

The work in the lab was interesting and my professional identity kept unfurling steadily, keeping company to the identity of myself as mother. Keeping company, supporting each other, limping along.

Carlos traveled extensively again and spent a lot of time in Peru and Argentina. Jason and I joined him often. The trips were a fascinating education for Jason and a welcome change for me. We traveled to Lago Victoria in Chile and watched with awe the lava-covered plains after a recent volcanic eruption. The demarcation line between the now cold lava and the green of the grass was shockingly sudden. With respect and reverence I picked up a small porous curd of lava and put it in my pocket, hoping that the universe would be kind to me and grant me the gift of feeling a part of it, a tiny but integral part of it again.

Climbing the heights to Machu Picchu, Jason got sick and needed oxygen. He had recovered by the next day and was eager to explore the ancient villages, wondering how the native boys could play soccer without getting sick in these rarified heights. We marveled at the walls built without any cement in the crevices and at the brilliant, inventive cutting of the stones that left no space in between. Jason's eagerness to see everything was infectious, his questions unending;

and my pride at his curiosity, a mixture of concern and encouragement, was as comfortable as old gloves.

I read voraciously in Spanish. The language was so beautiful, melodious, gentle, and yet decisive. Jason gave me a book of Antonio Machado's poetry for one of my birthdays, and we took turns reading it aloud. He recited as if on stage, and we competed in giving it strength and gentleness, not always sure of the meaning, but always sure of the intent.

Carlos was jealous of our closeness, Jason's and mine, but did not really know how to bridge the distance he, himself, had created. It was not clear whether he sincerely tried or just went through the motions. We traveled a lot, entertained a lot, and the commotions of daily life imprinted a definite restriction on my musings. It seemed there was less time to dedicate to sadness, feelings of rejection and loss of affection. But they were there in the background, never completely vanquished, never completely faded, a ghostly caricature on the good days, a mountainous heap of unhappiness on the bad days.

The collaboration with the Japanese gynecologist was scientifically successful, and eventually Carlos relented and let me travel to some local scientific meetings on my own to present the work I had found more and more absorbing. But my insecurities about public speaking returned, and I had to fight the lack of self-confidence, the anxiety, and my shyness, now in yet another language. International conferences were a bit easier, because the main language was English.

Interaction with European physicians and scientists was relaxed and comfortable. Many of them were women. I detected no need in them to sacrifice their femininity in order to succeed in their selected professions, and felt a sisterly connection with them that was invigorating. Their professional aspirations and lives were intact.

It was also easier to talk to male European physicians and scientists. There was a healthy camaraderie that reached beyond gender roles. Science and medicine were professional choices that did not include gender assignment. In groups we met for lunch and dinner, at night we went to clubs, and the peer acceptance was restorative. I traveled to Europe several times without too much resistance from Carlos, but he made sure that I did not attend any meeting in the United States, especially those in California.

Although I had opportunities to engage in journalism, I kept far away from it, petrified that it might push me into proximity with my failed career and thus, as improbable as it might seem, place me into dangerous zones of mutual interests with Will. A potentially shared domain with Will signified a threat to my sanity, to my integrity, to the new Will-less person I was frantically trying to become. Excursions into basic science with its logic, its factual pursuits of immunological mysteries of pregnancy in sheep, the unclothing of nature—it was all so much more worthwhile than self-absorbed, self-indulgent cravings for approval from uncaring men. Perhaps I was on the destructive path of subjugating my sexual and feminine identity to a professional one. The doubts about Will's professed love had never left me. The beautiful person I thought I was when I believed he loved me was an illusion. The femininity I felt was treacherous. I was damaged. Like the shards of a fragile vase, I had to be glued together. I could not be a cage suspended in midair, empty of life. I had to recreate the person of substance. I had to rebuild, evolve. I had to be a good mother, a skilled scientist. I had to survive.

The years passed slowly, one after another; the best years of my life, my lost thirties.

Five

Due to his advancing cancer, my father's condition worsened and we returned to New York. Carlos easily got his old job back after his exceptionally profitable years for the company while in Caracas. Their market had substantially expanded all over South America, thanks to Carlos. I was delighted to be back in New York and close to my family. And there were better schools for Jason, who was starting high school. Jason's educational prospects were the main reason Carlos agreed to return to the States. He was all in favor of good formal education, which Caracas was not able to provide. Carlos fully expected his son to enter an Ivy League institution and thus acquire an education that would guarantee professional success and affluence.

I used the opportunity to continue with my graduate studies, completing the requirements for a PhD in reproductive physiology. Given my years in the lab in Caracas, the immunology research, and the coauthored publications, the normal course of study was thankfully shortened.

The afternoon I successfully defended my doctoral

dissertation, I walked the streets looking at the buildings, the trees, and the people, listening to the traffic noises, eager to detect a sign of a life-altering change now that I had finally crossed the line and entered into this new identity, a person with a doctoral degree. The sky was the same vague blue with an occasional cloud, the leaves on the tree branches moved uncertainly in the wind, the traffic was just as noisy, the buildings wore the same tired facades. Nothing much had changed. I had a distinct feeling of acute disappointment that the rest of the world was not about to acknowledge the change in my professional status. So, I accepted with resignation and regret the anticlimax of it all. Some friends took me out to celebrate, but the idea that something of vital importance was still missing did not recede.

Carlos missed Caracas and used real and invented business reasons to go there. Soon he was spending more and more time there, where he purchased a large house with a pool. He found a private school for Jason that met the majority of his educational needs. So Jason and I returned to Caracas after my father died. Carlos was back in his element.

His jealousy abated, I even had my own car. My postdoc years were spent in the old lab, where my new professional status changed my work in small, hardly perceptible, ways. The research topics were familiar, with a slightly increased emphasis on viral infections. Seminar discussions yielded meager new avenues of approach and the methodology was basically unchanged, despite new technology that was incorporated as it became available. Each new publication was a slight variation of the previous one. I felt unchallenged and stifled with little progress. Years rolled by, lazily. Jason was in his senior year in high school and would soon enter college, I hoped, in the States.

As soon as Jason finished high school, I left Carlos and went back to New York. The departure was caused by a quarrel, when I bought two pairs of sandals without asking permission for the purchase. Carlos almost choked me. My leaving was, and was not, premeditated.

There are specific sources of information available to those looking for jobs in the sciences. Most scientific journals carry advertisements for open research and academic positions, but the best source is a scientific conference. At a conference one can get an immediate interview with the prospective employers, and the entire process is streamlined and direct.

At the next international conference in my field, I looked at the job opportunities, especially those in New York. It was my town and I hoped that I still had friends there. It was also familiar, a safer pool to jump into; not as deep and as turbulent as if I launched myself into completely new surroundings, where everything would be strange and unfamiliar, including the streets and neighborhoods, little shops, department stores and, of course, people. I particularly did not want to go someplace where there was no public transportation, because I doubted I had enough money saved to buy a car. I knew I would need what money I had for a security deposit and a month's rent for an apartment, before I could count on any salary. In New York I had friends and I planned to ask to stay with one of them for a few weeks, before I found an apartment. Carlos had let me use one department store credit card, which was in his name but had my signature. I was hoping I could continue using the card once I had a new billing address.

The conference meeting I went to in search of a job was in Caracas, but it had posted teaching and research opportunities all over the United States, including a few in New York City. I was extremely lucky in my first attempt, a teaching and research position at a college that was part of the large state university system. I applied for the job in the morning and had the interview that afternoon. The person advertising for the position, the head of a small research lab in reproductive physiology, knew some of the people I had worked with in Caracas and also my doctoral thesis advisor. Apparently he valued my prior experience sufficiently to offer me the job on the spot. I even detected a degree of encouragement when I confessed that I wanted out of my marriage and was looking to relocate to New York City. He volunteered a piece of his own personal plight, telling me that he was separated from his wife. I wondered if he told me that thinking I was an easy lay? It is possible, but when he offered the job starting the following September, I took it. The teaching load would consist of teaching a course in general anatomy and physiology for nurses, while the research obligations included supervising his graduate students' research. There was potential for starting my own research projects, if I agreed to write grant proposals to obtain research funds. It was not a tenure-track position, but it sounded encouraging. What I liked best was that it was in New York.

When Carlos left on one of his longer business trips in August, I packed several suitcases with clothes, books, and papers I thought I would need to prepare my lectures. One of my friends, Paula, who was director of the engineering lab at Columbia University and had a two-bedroom apartment, let me stay in one of the bedrooms for a few weeks. Shortly after I arrived, she left for a European vacation. I was alone in her large apartment with a fully stocked refrigerator and a glorious view of the Hudson River.

She asked few questions and accepted my reasons for leaving Carlos without as much as a question mark or even a shrug. I realized she was silently acknowledging that it was high time I left Carlos. We were not close friends; I was closer to her sister. She had recently divorced her husband, who was also from South America – Argentina, I thought - and had been a friend of Carlos's. Perhaps her sister's divorce added to Paula's understanding of my plight. In any case, I appreciated her discretion and her help.

I spent the next several days looking for an apartment. Finding an affordable apartment in the neighborhoods I chose was not easy, but walking the streets of the city alone, with so much hope in every step, filled me with a sense of freedom and with energy I did not know I possessed.

After two weeks I found an apartment within walking distance of the college. It was a pleasant one-bedroom apartment on the top floor of a semi-attached building that looked like a townhouse and had an elevator. The living room was not big but had two large windows overlooking the fire escape and the street. The tiny kitchen included a stove, sink, a small refrigerator, and some cabinets. The bathroom was reached through a small bedroom whose window opened onto a dark air shaft between the buildings.

I looked forward to furnishing it to my taste, entirely to my taste, without having to check with Carlos, without his righteous scrutiny. Since it was about twenty blocks from the college, I hoped I could walk to work and would not have to spend money on transportation. It was a long walk, but it was summer and snow and slush were future hazards. The first thing I purchased was a bar stool with a cane seat, which for some strange reason seemed irresistible. I brought it home on the subway. And, yes, I still have it. The proof of my first foray into independence, a relic from the time of change and transition.

As soon as Paula returned from her European vacation, I showed her my new apartment, borrowed a cot from her, and let her sit on the cane barstool. She brought a bottle of Portuguese rosé to celebrate and we drank from the bottle, because I had no glasses. We laughed and laughed between each other's turn at the bottle.

"Should have thought of bringing glasses," Paula said in between gulps. "And you don't even have a toothbrush glass like any other normal person." She was laughing so hard, tears filled her eyes.

The rest of the living room furniture, a dining room table and four chairs, and a sofa bed for Jason I bought on credit using Carlos's department store credit card. He never found out I used it and that it helped in building my credit. My mother generously gave me enough money to open a checking account. It felt as if I had suddenly acquired a new identity. My life was just starting at the age of forty. It took almost twenty more years until I bought bedroom furniture, but I did not know then what was in store for me in the future.

I kept walking the streets, looking at the apartment houses, even in the most familiar neighborhoods, as if their facades were newly rinsed and newly clothed. I took in everything happening on the streets, jealously guarding it as if afraid I would be robbed of each new sound or novel smell. I was discovering the city as if on an adventure, as if everything was freshly baked, decorated like a birthday cake with thousands of flickering candles. I walked through Central Park smiling at the mothers with kids in their strollers, old and young couples holding hands and eating ice cream, people walking their dogs. All those who, like I, were an elemental part of this glorious gift of nature, summer in New York.

Although it was August and the days were hot, it was not humid, and it did not remind me of Caracas. I did not mind the jostling crowds of tourists on Fifth Avenue, proud of being again a part of this lively city—free, without deadlines or any responsibilities, no need to give accounts of where I was headed or where I had been. No need for any explanations, excuses, apologies, or approvals. Just a simple unencumbered way of life, devoid of all reproach, pretense, or regret. The feeling of being on vacation was exhilarating. I felt so light that I could fly.

Skipping up the steps to the entrance of the Museum of Natural History, I was elated at the prospect of seeing only those exhibits I really wanted to see. There would be no impatient tugs on my sleeve as Carlos wanted to abandon the mineral exhibit and hurry to astronomy. I could spend an hour looking at the jewelry made by this or that African tribe. I could leisurely compare the social organization of ants to that of bees and termites.

My legs achy and tired after long afternoons in the Metropolitan Museum, I kept returning for more. There was always more to see. I felt guilty for abandoning it each day and for not having visited it for years. When I really could not walk anymore, I would sit in those rooms with benches and slowly turn to look at each painting for as long as I wanted, trying to figure out the painter's motivation in painting the portrait of this man or of that woman. Rembrandt's portraits were true to nature, using a palette of dark colors, but there was nothing fearsome or anxiety provoking in the faces of people he painted. Goya's portraits frightened me. Picasso's I did not always understand. No, not understand. I did not fully appreciate the broken lines, the virtue of the diagrammatic, almost purely ascetic form. I wanted warmth, softness, not angularity. I spent hours in front of an expressionist painting by Feininger in the Museum of Modern Art, because his style reminded me of another painter, Miljenko Stancic, who painted with similar muted colors the roofs and steeples of my hometown.

I stood in front of the Tiffany store on Fifth Avenue, admiring the beautiful displays of precious jewels hidden in between little branches, sparkling with hope, greeting my smile with its own brilliant brightness, a smile in response to mine. A dialogue of smiles between me and my city, a dialogue of hope, independence, autonomy. A dialogue of freedom.

I walked a lot: one day through the Village, the next through Chinatown, the next up and down Madison Avenue. I wished I could tell my European friends that Madison Avenue shops were more interesting and filled with just as fashionable clothes as any in Milan or Paris. New Yorkers rushed around me, walking with purpose, impatient on the escalators, while I walked without apparent aim, open to the city, taking pleasure in having no particular goal.

After a few days I noticed that my skirts danced around my waist. I had lost a lot of weight, almost fifteen pounds, without noticing. I definitely felt lighter, having shed the weight of my marriage, my responsibilities, and some of my past. It was invigorating. I did not have money to buy a new wardrobe, but it did not matter, because the loose clothes were less constrictive. I had never felt such freedom, with so much hope for the future. It was the summer of the highest expectations. Life was defined in terms of possibilities.

My new boss seemed likable, and when he asked me to start with the research part of my job immediately, I agreed. As soon as I met his three graduate students, it was clear that they were all behind in their research. His lab was well equipped but far from the technology I was used to in Caracas. In Caracas we'd had easy access to other labs for histology and electron microscopy; to electricians and carpenters. I never questioned their existence and expected their willing help as a matter of course. But such collaborative help in New York needed funds. Everything not in the actual lab required a requisition. The grant money was tight. There was a lot of paperwork and lots of rejected requests. The graduate students were relatively inept and inexperienced around the lab. We had to make our own repairs to the laboratory equipment. I carried a screwdriver in my lab coat at all times. In Caracas I was expected to make most of my own microelectrodes, but in New York I had to make them for the graduate students as well because theirs never worked. They were very creative with their explanations of why their experiments failed and why no valid data got collected, when it was clear to me that it was due to low motivation and their obvious lack of perseverance. When things did not work the first time, they often gave up, and I had to cajole them like little children to get them to try again. They resented failures and did not have the patience to overcome even the slightest of obstacles.

When I designed a Plexiglas chamber as part of our experimental setup, which was needed for some new measurements, there were no shop facilities to make it according to my design. Since Paula worked at the Columbia engineering school, I begged her for help. She willingly agreed, but we had to work on it and test it in her lab at night, when none of her associates were present. My boss approved of my resourcefulness, but the graduate students resented it. They resented me—this new impediment placed between the boss and them—and the additional step of approval. Used to hard work, the seriousness of the Caracas lab and its success, I expected a lot of myself, and they thought I pushed them too hard. One of them, Celine, a girl who babysat for the boss, was especially resentful. She kept quiet when I asked her to do things or when I asked why certain tasks were not completed. Later, regaining her full verbal capacity, she complained to the boss behind my back, exaggerating the issues. I considered it beneath my dignity to acknowledge a problem or ever argue my side of the story.

The other graduate student, Michael, belonged to a rock band and had lots of weekend engagements that left him totally incapacitated on Mondays. He would come in late, high on weed or whatever else he was taking, in smelly clothes and definitely not showered, and completely uninterested in reproductive physiology on the cellular level. The problem was that Monday was one of his two days in the lab, and he typically spent it recuperating or sleeping in the little cubicle adjacent to his lab. Around three o'clock in the afternoon, he would wake up and disappear to get something to eat, and then complain when I asked him not to eat his soup or drink his coffee next to the computer keyboard or the experimental setup.

"Alex," he would start in a loud voice. He knew that I resented being called *Alex*. "I don't care shit about my MS degree in biology! But my parents don't pay the rent and my allowance if I don't pass exams."

For Michael, getting a masters in science seemed the best way to pacify his parents and let him pursue a musical career without jeopardizing his financial support. When sober and not on drugs, he was exceptionally intelligent, and could have been a superlative student if he just had the motivation. He was actually a nice, good-natured person who could converse eloquently on a variety of topics, because he read anything at hand. His awareness of current events was remarkable. We often argued about poetry and lent each other novels to read. His knowledge of biology, physics, and math was outstanding and thorough. He passed his written tests admirably well. It was just when it came to experimental lab work—which was unfortunately required for his masters—that he showed no interest. I tried to motivate him and spent hours talking with him. We were the best of friends as long as I did not force him into the lab to conduct experiments.

The teaching part of my job did not go smoothly either. I encountered problems at the very beginning. The college had open admissions into the first year, and my class was huge. I lectured with a microphone and a projector instead of a blackboard to more than three hundred prospective nurses. The final exams were supposed to fail 80 percent of the students, because the second year had places for only about sixty. It seemed extremely unfair: why give false hope to so many with free admission, throw them unprepared into the water, and expect them to swim? The textbook was a familiar standard text, but the tests I was supposed to give included questions not covered in the textbook. I felt a responsibility to cover those additional topics in my lectures, which made the students unhappy. They could not find the content of my lectures in the textbook and kept interrupting me with questions. In order to also cover the standard text content, the lectures often ran longer. When I tried to change the test questions on some of the exams, my teaching assistants complained, because now they had to readjust the answer keys to correct the tests.

One of the teaching assistants was an obese woman in her late fifties who was permanently ensconced in a size smaller, brilliantly white starched lab coat that she proudly laundered and ironed herself. She was an MD with foreign credentials. She had failed to pass the board exams in order to practice medicine in the States and worked as a teaching assistant due to her former academic experience in Bulgaria. She had been an orthopedic specialist in her native country and believed that she knew everything there was to know about bones. My lectures on bone formation covered the most recent research findings on the cellular and molecular aspects of bone formation, including some simple biochemistry, which most likely had not been known during her student days. That she was not familiar with the most recent research didn't surprise me; it was probably why she had not passed her board exams. Content with the knowledge she possessed, seeing no need to keep up with the literature, she flatly refused to change any test questions dealing with bone formation. She argued that the molecular aspects of bone formation were beyond the comprehension of the first-year nursing students anyway.

The original test questions were entirely devoted to the gross anatomy of bones, which had not changed in recent years. The more recent findings in microstructure, however, were fascinating, and I felt it might motivate some of the future nurses to read the original articles in the professional journals. The Bulgarian MD had been a teaching assistant for many years, had taught all anatomy lab sections dealing with bones, and felt that it was her right to continue with the same strategy. She stubbornly resisted any changes, and her criticism and resentfulness of me was palpable.

"You are new," she would say. "This is not how we do things here. The change is not always for the better. The nurses need to know the basic anatomy and physiology. The biochemistry is too difficult for them. They will never use this knowledge in their practice. Why make life difficult? Why make life difficult for me and for them? You know what they say about a new broom, right?"

Yes, I was new, but I also wanted to be more than an average teacher. The microstructure of the bones could be a fascinating subject. Why shouldn't the future nurses learn biochemistry? Perhaps not all of them would be intrigued by the scientific mysteries of the bones, but surely some would want to know more.

My teaching initiatives were not appreciated. With the teaching troubles escalating even further when the new tests did not fail enough students, in addition to the troubles with the graduate students in the lab, I started to suspect that my contract with the college would not be renewed. The second semester confirmed my suspicions. After having failed to fail enough nursing students, I was given a different teaching assignment. Now I was teaching introductory biology courses and their labs. This was a definite demotion. On the other hand, I was not too unhappy, because the courses for nurses were evening courses. It was usually around eleven o'clock at night when I finally collected my notes, overheads, and colored pens, stuffed them into my bag, and started toward the subway to go home.

The walk to the subway took me through several deserted blocks on the Lower East Side where several months earlier there had been a rape. The young woman was also severely beaten and died in the hospital. This part of the city was populated by the homeless, most of them drug addicts and former psychiatric patients who did not even bother to beg. They just lay there, dropped out of the hospital as a result of the decrease in government funds for mental care. I was grateful when some of the male nursing students offered to accompany me on the walk to the subway. On more than one occasion even the Guardian Angels walked me to the subway, and I struck a friendship with them.

"Hi, Doc!" they'd greet me. "How's it going? Shall we walk you home tonight?"

Surrounded by their confident, smiling faces and bulging biceps clearly visible through their freshly laundered white T-shirts, I felt safe and secure. The subways were not any safer than the streets in those times either, but the ride was short and the Guardian Angels in their red berets waited with me on the subway platform until the train arrived. They waved good-bye as the doors closed.

In June, when my one-year contract with the college expired, I was unemployed. For the next six months I collected unemployment. I also learned that if I got a part-time job and earned a small salary—not enough to support myself—the unemployment checks would be reduced. I put a lot of effort into the letter to accompany my curriculum vitae and applied for more than three hundred jobs. As instructed by my well-meaning friends, I would send my letter and the CV and then follow up with a phone call a week later. Of course, I felt that I was qualified for all the jobs I applied for, but there were no interviews. Once when I followed up the application with the phone call, I was told that they did not call me, because my name sounded too foreign. Since nobody knew how to pronounce it, they did not call me for an interview. They did not want a biology teacher who could not speak English and were pleasantly surprised that I could, indeed, speak English and had an impressive CV, but the teaching job, regrettably, was no longer available.

Unemployment is demoralizing. It pushed me into long sessions with myself, analyzing the causes and reasons. To what degree had it been my fault and what should I have done to prevent it? I vacillated between days of optimism, telling myself that I was better educated than the job had required and that my next job would be an improvement. Getting that job had allowed me to get out of a failed marriage and leave Carlos. That was a good thing. Losing the job was an opportunity to look for something better. There were also days of despair when it was hard to get up in the morning and write yet another cover letter or fill out yet another job application … But this first onslaught on my professional identity was not fatal, just a dent. Optimism prevailed, and life would again offer possibilities. Or so I thought.

I became superstitious and picked up coins from the streets, believing they would bring me luck. I would store them in a little purse and keep count of them, hoping to use them on a subway ride for the next job interview. The stash of found coins and more than a few subway tokens grew steadily, unused.

My mother helped with the rent expenses, and I got a sort of grant for an electronics course as a condition to continue receiving unemployment benefits. My previous research had involved a fair amount of electronic equipment, and judging by the past year's experience in the lab, when I'd had to do my own repairs, it seemed prudent to learn enough electronics to repair my own lab equipment. It was an easy semester-long electronics course, geared to reeducate those without skills and—I soon realized—those without college degrees. Needless to say I kept my PhD degree and the fact that I had taught college-level courses a secret. There were thirty-two students; the majority were recent high school graduates. Most were males and they regarded me as their big sister. The atmosphere was friendly and we helped each other complete each exercise. My most frequent job was to read the instruction manuals while they performed various other tasks under my guidance. The course was not without benefits. I learned basic electronics, computer hardware and repair, and fundamentals of software commands, all of which I found fascinating. Tracing the signals through various computer components, once I understood how they operated, was not difficult. There was no Internet yet. The computers were bigger and by comparison to contemporary iPhones, iPods, and iPads, clumsier, with easily removable motherboards and easily replaceable electronic units.

I did not share my fascination with electronics with my friends. Paula knew, but believed it a glorious waste of time, given my other credentials. She kept me company during some depressing evenings and suggested other job possibilities. My other friends also had suggestions for finding work. None were especially constructive. One of them, a busy mother of two, a lapsed pianist married to a jazz musician, offered to find me work as a dog walker. I declined.

Another of my friends, who was currently going through therapy, urged me to advertise as a therapist. In her opinion, one did not need a doctoral degree to be a therapist. Her therapist just sat and listened and hardly ever talked. Some of our conversations, she said, were more useful to her than the sessions with her therapist. And she was paying lots of money for these, according to her, totally unproductive sessions. She thought that being a therapist was an easy and lucrative profession and that I was a fool for not attempting it, especially since my life had supplied me with enough experience to give good advice.

"Really, Alexandra, I don't understand your reluctance to advertise as a therapist."

"But in order to be a therapist you need to be trained. You need a license," I protested.

"But you have a doctorate. Isn't that enough?"

I was discouraged by her lack of understanding, but was grateful when she offered a substantial loan and kept inviting me out for dinner or lunch, and to many of her parties. She was an excellent cook, had interesting friends, and I felt privileged to be invited.

During this bout of unemployment, I discovered that cooking could be a creative enterprise. I would buy whole chickens on sale and prepare numerous meals out of the one bird, using innards and necks to make soups, stewing legs, thighs, and wings, and roasting the breasts one at a time, with leftover pieces in sandwiches or salads. Rice and pasta were affordable, and so were eggs. There were many rice-and-beans, pasta-and-salad meatless days.

The fruits from tropical climates, ones that were so cheap and plentiful in Venezuela, were prohibitively expensive in New York. I would wistfully eye the mangoes, pineapples, and kiwis, but bought only those fruits and vegetables that were in season. Venezuelans were smart and well-fed on rice, beans, and plantains, a perfectly balanced meal without meat. But no matter how I tried, I could not become a vegetarian. After several days without meat, I would crave it and cook a pork chop, and then I would balance the budgetary lapse with more rice. Passing by the fruit and vegetable stores, I would scan the offerings, seeking items on sale and passing over mushrooms, kiwis, strawberries, and pineapple. Although in my childhood raspberries were plentiful, in New York I could not afford them. Bananas were affordable, but I patiently waited for the fall when the apples from upstate New York would appear. I bought a basketful that would last me for months. I became adept at spotting any food on sale or any specials. I never ate out, never even had a slice of pizza or a cup of coffee. It was cheaper to make a sandwich at home. Luckily I liked eggs and beans and bought differently shaped pasta, so it would not always be spaghetti. Very often it was pasta with a stew of vegetables, onions, carrots, celery, an occasional zucchini, spiced with herbs and lots of paprika, which gave the dish an appealing reddish color.

At the time people did not drink a lot of bottled water, but they did drink a variety of sodas. I had no money for soda. Every morning I would boil water, drop a tea bag into a cup for hot tea, and then use the same tea bag to make a small pitcher of lighter tea. If I had some orange juice or a lemon—which rarely fit my budget—I would add orange juice or squeeze drops of lemon into the pitcher to drink the rest of the day as iced tea. The custom became so strong that I still do this, although now, of course, I can afford fresh oranges and lemons, and raspberries to my heart's content.

I kept reading the Sunday edition of the *New York Times* and *Science* magazine, looking for jobs. This was not the time of e-mails and easy electronic communication. Job applications traveled by ordinary mail. And I kept revising my cover letter and my CV to tailor them to each new job opening. Eventually I saw an ad for a research associate at a graduate school. I immediately applied and was invited for an interview.

During my months of unemployment I'd had lots of free time, and I partially filled it with free yoga and jazz exercise classes at neighborhood high schools. I felt in great shape physically and looked years younger than when I lived in Caracas. I dressed with care for the interview, wearing one of the two wool suits I had acquired for that purpose and which had hung in the closet unused. The suit was a subdued plaid of green, blue, and beige. I wore my only beige silk blouse, which had also hung unworn in the closet for a long time. No jewelry except for my favorite gold earrings, a present from Carlos.

As I entered the room to be interviewed, a man rose to greet me, extended his hand for a handshake. He suddenly stopped and threw both arms in a wide gesture, grinning.

"Why, Alexandra, you decided on a matching suit for this interview?"

I must have looked momentarily startled, not

understanding his comment, but then I noticed that he was dressed in a suit in an almost identical color pattern as mine.

"You don't mind being on a first name basis?" he continued. "I am Jeff. And I really like your suit."

Recovering from the initial surprise, I said, "No, not at all. Pleased to meet you Jeff." Now I was laughing. "And I really like *your* suit!"

I'm not sure to what extent my professional experience counted, but I am sure I got the job because of the suit I wore. What a fortuitous choice it had been!

I soon learned that I was not the only new hire. A woman psychologist had also been hired and I would be sharing an office with her. Jeff suggested that we meet informally before starting work to see whether we got along.

I invited Susan, the psychologist, for lunch at my apartment. I planned to serve open-faced Swiss cheese sandwiches on pumpernickel, vegetable soup I had prepared myself, and my staple, iced tea. Simple, civilized, grown-up fare.

Susan was petite, wore an old-fashioned cotton dress, although it was the middle of winter, had no make-up, and blushed as she talked about herself. She impressed me as a shy person, willing to please and be liked. She said she was married to a lawyer and then immediately added that although they had been married for over six years, they had no children, despite a continued effort. Somewhat startled by this breathless, uninhibited confession, I wondered why she appeared so shy and insecure if she had such a healthy sex life. At that moment I envied her sex life, even as I nodded in support and tried to put her at ease. She talked a lot during lunch, which soon was not a meal at all. She never touched the sandwich, and hardly had more than a spoonful of soup, but drank a tall glass of iced tea in great thirsty gulps.

"Susan, would you like more tea?" She extended her glass and I poured her more tea. "Don't you like the sandwich? Would you like something else?"

"No, no, the sandwich is fine, I guess. If you can call it a sandwich. But it looks strange, don't you think, with the cheese so exposed? I'm not used to seeing the cheese in a sandwich."

"Well, that is easily remedied. I do have more bread. Let me cover the cheese... with another slice of bread. Would you like that?" I got up to get another slice of bread from the kitchenette.

The exposed cheese now covered, she seemed relieved and took a bite. She chewed thoughtfully, as if testing it, and upon finding it palatable, swallowed.

She tried to turn the conversation to my personal life, but I resisted. I did tell her that I had left my husband and then switched the topic to more appropriate professional grounds and talked about my research. Susan seemed bored and did not reciprocate.

When Jeff called the next day to tell me that all the formalities were in order and I could start the new job the following Monday, he asked about lunch with Susan. I lied and said, "The lunch was fine." But Susan had already called him.

"Susan said you were so *European*. You served open-faced sandwiches, such a novelty for her. Yes, she said she would be delighted to share the office with you."

I should have sensed that something was not right with

Susan and me sharing an office when she found me so odd, so foreign. I really, really wanted that job—needed that job—so I dismissed all potential worries. But I should have known better than to share an office with an insecure, neurotic, frustrated, and suspicious person. She listened to my phone calls and wanted to know who I talked to, and then made comments about the conversations. Her profile seemed etched in unabashed, misdirected rectitude.

"Who was that on the phone?" she would ask.

"Jeff."

"Isn't this a second time he called today? You talk to Jeff at lot, don't you?"

"Yes, we are working on a book chapter."

"Aren't you lucky? Writing a book chapter with Jeff. He hasn't asked me to write a chapter with him yet, but we were discussing a topic that would make a great book chapter."

"That's great, Susan."

"But do you think you have enough material already for a book chapter?"

When I added a new picture of Jason to my desk, Susan noticed right away. "Who is that handsome young man you have there? Your boyfriend?"

"No, this is my son Jason. He just started college."

"Aren't you lucky to have a child? And so grown up already. And in college! Where does he go to school? What does he study?"

"Jason is in Philadelphia. He hasn't selected his major yet."

"Do you think he will study biology like you?"

"I'm not sure. I don't think so."

"Do you miss him? You don't talk on the phone often, do you? Does he visit?"

"Yes, I miss him, and, yes, we talk on the phone, and, yes, he visits."

Susan insisted on locking the office when it was empty, although everybody else left their offices open and unlocked during the day. This was very inconvenient for me. I worked in the lab on a different floor and often needed to go to the office numerous times during the day. If she wasn't there, I had to unlock the door to enter and then lock it upon exiting, because Susan would complain if she found the door unlocked.

It was not easy to avoid socializing with each other, since we both ate lunch at our desks most days, but it was a strained and superficial friendship, compounded by my resentment of the fact that our salaries were comparable. We both had PhDs, but I had so much more research experience and was older. Jeff explained that we started at the same time in similar positions, as research associates, and that my former experience did not make a difference.

Jeff often came to talk to me in my office whether Susan was present or not, and at other times we met in his office to design studies, analyze data, or discuss the significance of the most recent findings. Jeff valued my opinions and our collaboration was straightforward, unencumbered by any prejudice. Susan was extremely jealous of this and constantly asked me why Jeff preferred working with me.

Susan and I were both expected to write research grant proposals to provide for a major part of our salaries as research associates. The grant applications had deadlines and were expected to be based on previous research results. It became a vicious circle: design a study with minimal funds and then collect data as soon as possible to use it in a research proposal to secure more funds to continue doing research.

For the eight years that I spent doing that, my social life was nonexistent. If I was not running experiments or analyzing data, I was writing yet another research grant proposal. The proposals were submitted to local funding agencies in the hope that the funds would provide studies with results warranting a NIH proposal. In the beginning I was required to provide funds for 60 percent of my salary. As time went on, I was slowly but steadily promoted to a tenure-track position as an assistant professor and then as an associate professor. I wrote five substantial NIH grant proposals. None were rejected for funding, but were recommended for funding with priority scores that were too low to get the grants funded. NIH had limited funds. The grants with highest priority scores were funded first, often receiving the full 100 percent of the requested funds. Many grants recommended for funding never received any, since NIH ran out of money by the time they were under review. To have a research grant proposal with a priority score eligible for funding and not funded could be a good thing, because you could reapply the next year and by introducing new data, hope for a higher priority score with a greater chance of being funded.

All of my NIH grant proposals kept being recommended for funding. I kept revising them, kept running new studies... At every opportunity I talked to my colleagues at scientific meetings to get new insights and to secure permission to include their yet unpublished data in support of my own finding for yet another revised proposal. I kept writing research grant proposals during evenings and nights and weekends to meet the relentless deadlines for submission.

In addition to writing grant proposals, I carried a full teaching load of at least one, and often two, graduate seminars each semester. And there was the committee work. I chaired one committee and was member of two others. The committee work was time consuming, seldom rewarding. Actually, quite often it was a waste of time. Over the years several students received their graduate degrees under my advisory supervision.

None of it helped in the end. After six years of being an associate professor, I was refused promotion to full professor and failed to get tenure, primarily because I was unsuccessful in obtaining NIH research funds and had not published enough. The grants I did receive from the local funding agencies were not sufficient to provide 60 percent of my salary. I had dreamed of becoming tenured, hoping that the grant-writing time would be over and I would reenter normal life, going to the movies and the theater, a meal out with friends, and, yes, dating!

During the feverish grant-writing years, my social life deteriorated into nonexistence. It was limited to scientific conferences, some of them international and in exotic places, where the hotel rooms and meals were covered by the institution. Having done your job as a contributing scientist, you had a panel presentation, a talk or a poster, and you could relax, laugh with your colleagues, dance, and stay out late and party. Those twice-a-year occasions for fun motivated hard work during the year just as much as the need for research funds. Without new data, new results to report, one could not write a revision of a grant, but more important—one could not send an abstract, the summary of performed research studies, to an annual meeting, thus missing all the fun.

One of the annual scientific meetings took place at a Florida beach resort in May of each year. This was the perfect time to visit Florida. I made sure I had a completed study and an abstract ready for this conference, not only because it was an international meeting and quite prestigious, but because apart from a short presentation of my research findings, I could spend the rest of the time at the beach.

If the presentation was a talk, it was a bit more anxiety provoking for me because of the larger audience, but since no talk was allowed to be longer than ten minutes, it was quickly over. Scientific presentations are scrupulously structured. Presenters have to make a brief, relevant introduction, state the objective of the study, describe the methods, the results, and end with a clear conclusion. The result section is the most important part and it is usually the longest, with graphs, tables, charts or other such figures. The conclusion is equally as important, because it might lead to further investigations and promising new studies.

If the presentation at the conference is a poster, one has to sacrifice at least half a day to stand in front of it and answer questions from the passing throng of inquiring minds. It is more prestigious to have your research study selected for a talk than a poster presentation, but the posters are ultimately more scientifically profitable. From the questions of other scientists doing similar research, one gleans novel ideas and new approaches to the same problems. Their questions can identify snags and pitfalls of an approach that their research already exposed, thus saving you from similar errors. It is customary for one of the authors to be present at the poster for such discussions at least during a designated hour, but the rest of the presentation time—which is normally three to four hours per poster session—one can visit other posters and chat with other authors. The poster sessions are organized by topics and subtopics. The location of each poster within a session is assigned by number, and their abstracts appear in the accompanying books at each conference. Inexperienced young scientists with a meager list of publications to their credit often list the abstracts of conference presentations as part of their bibliographies to enhance their scientific acumen, but seasoned scientists do not resort to such gimmicks. Such practice is deemed unethical. Only publications in peer-reviewed journals count when cited in the bibliography.

Susan was extremely jealous that most of my conference presentations and the eventual research grant proposals were in collaboration with Jeff. Because of his clinical responsibilities, he contributed only a meager part to the general endeavor, but he was a full professor with considerable influence at the college. At the conferences, he proudly stood in front of our poster and answered questions for about fifteen minutes and then disappeared "to view the competition." That often included lengthy discussions with female scientists having a drink at the bar or on the beach. He was an attractive man whose wife never traveled with him to any of the meetings. He used the time to chat up the attractive graduate students or postdocs. He regularly hosted end-of-conference parties in his lavish hotel room that lasted long into the night. They were quite famous for the plentiful alcohol and lots of shrimp. Jeff liked shrimp. As I was invariably the first author on our projects—I initiated most of them—I was always invited to his parties. Susan was not always invited, depending on the size of the party and whether it included all faculty or was just a private Jeff party. I suspected that institutional funds were always used to cover the expenses and that the parties were labeled as promoting research interests of the institution. I went for the shrimp and a glass of wine but never stayed too long, since they deteriorated into weed-smoking free-for-all. Susan, I suspected, would have liked staying to the end, so she could gossip about who left with whom after the party. I was silent in the face of her insistent interrogations about what the party was like, if she did not attend. I divulged nothing of any interest, even keeping some entertaining details to myself out or pure spite. One or two times, Susan asked me to take her when she wasn't invited herself. I obliged and later regretted the creative gossip she disseminated about my fellow scientists, deserving or not. In the beginning Susan and I shared a hotel room, but later I paid for my own room and avoided her during the conference as much as possible. Because of her fair skin Susan hated the beach, so at least there I was totally safe. The subject matter of her research did not overlap with mine sufficiently for her to be a coauthor, and I was eternally grateful for that.

Susan was not promoted or tenured either. I heard she left for a job out of New York, but I persisted in looking for another job in the New York area, hating the idea of leaving the city. There was a job opening at the medical school in St. Louis, but I did not apply for it and remained unemployed yet again.

I chose to believe that the failure to get tenure and keep my job was not a personal failure, but was due to unfavorable circumstances. I still had a great desire to succeed professionally and I viewed my second unemployment as a temporary setback. Introspective self-analysis started again as I examined the causes and reasons for failure. But I really did not blame myself.

With confidence, I listed my professional assets: I was well educated, had graduate and postgraduate training, a doctorate from a reputable institution, and publications in peer-reviewed journals. I had research and teaching experience. I was still young ... Well, let us say, I was not inexperienced. On the other hand, federal funds for research were difficult to obtain, competition was fierce. My grant proposals had scientific merit and were recommended for funding. They just weren't funded. It was not exactly my fault that the NIH lacked sufficient funds for all meritorious proposals. It was not my fault that the research funds were so scarce.

The previous years kept me too busy with grant writing to have much of a social life or to enjoy the city I loved. I was determined not to look for a similar job again. I was not completely sure whether to abandon academia. I liked teaching and doing research, but did not want to be dependent again on "soft" grant money. I wanted less uncertainty in my future professional life—a set salary, health insurance, vacations ... Continuity. In my next job, I hoped to be in control of my time. The life—I still viewed the life—in terms of possibilities. I was not ready for the disappointments when those possibilities remained just that, possibilities. The optimism was still there. I had been unemployed once and survived. I would survive it again. Practice made perfect.

In the meantime, Jason had finished college and graduate school. He visited on weekends as often as his studies permitted. Sometimes he would bring his laundry and sometimes he would study the whole weekend, but generally he spent time in New York willingly. Needless to say, the city was rich with opportunities for entertainment and diversion. He and his friends were happy to explore. Having a place to stay while in New York was an advantage. We had long debates and conversations on a variety of topics related to his studies and my research and, of course, the meaning of life. Jason was still a voracious reader and interested in just about everything. He could be just as passionate about basketball as about the history and philosophy of science. He had superb analytical skills and his discourse seldom lacked convincing evidence. We did not always agree and argued often; he unwilling to admit that my views had merit, I unwilling to admit that I often learned from him. At times he brought his friends for dinner. We would all engage in lively discussions, which occasionally deteriorated into mild confrontations of opposing views, the generational gap between us overt and palpable. Or I would listen to anecdotes of their college adventures.

When my busy schedule allowed, Jason accompanied me to the theater and to exhibitions at the Museum of Modern Art or the Guggenheim. I was grateful for every moment he spent with me, because at his age, being with his mother was certainly not a priority. During those rare, private inner moments, I prayed that our effortless companionship would never change.

Jason also visited his father, who was financing his education. They were finally developing a relationship. Though he had never been good at talking to children, including his own son, Carlos could relate to an adult. At the end of his graduate studies, Jason met his future wife. They were an attractive couple, very much in love. Carlos gave them a big engagement party, to which I was invited and happily attended. And soon Jason married. This was just about the time I was denied tenure and left academia. I suppose both of us were embarking on a new voyage—but his waters proved to be calmer than mine.

Halfheartedly returning to the idea of journalism and writing, I took an intensive workshop on magazine writing, planning to use my scientific background to write about science. The somewhat cavalier attitude toward facts, the simplified approach to issues coupled with flimsy documentation, needed for a magazine article surprised me. Having been trained in research with its rigorousness, the need for supporting evidence, and demand for accurate attribution of each source of information proved to be impossible obstacles. Used to writing scientific articles for professional journals, I was unwilling to compromise. My articles were judged too stuffy, too full of details that no reader would appreciate or have the patience to read. Magazine writing required little in the way of documentation of facts. All one needed was to quote a well-known scientist; or rather, to paraphrase what he had said in language comprehensible to the general public. It was important to spell his name correctly and note the date of the interview. Any potentially fascinating detail or a deeper scientific insight did not need to be explained, just mentioned and superficially described.

The full, convoluted chronology of the scientific effort to elucidate a problem was seldom examined. The original inquiry, the objective, was of secondary importance. Only the conclusion—the bottom line—mattered. Science was presented as a string of events and not of insights or accomplishments.

Prior to the magazine workshop, I had this naïve vision of making science comprehensible and palatable to those without scientific training. When I read magazine articles about the "latest" discovery or an account of some issues discussed at a recent scientific conference written by writers without a scientific background, I often felt embarrassed by their lack of knowledge. It was not the style that was disturbing. Magazine writing allowed much more freedom of expression and was far less structured than scientific writing. It was the realization that the writer had missed the point of a core controversy through ignorance of some basic scientific fact and the public was being misinformed. The goal of magazine writing was to report and entertain, grab the attention of the ignorant public with exaggerated claims of success or by invented potential dangers of a benign discovery, while I wished it to be educational. But exaggeration sold the magazines. Mere facts were boring or required further reading of even more boring material. Who had time for that? Knowledge must be desired or it fails to educate.

Many trivial misconceptions about science have been propagated through shows on television and in films for the sake of entertainment. Scientists are portrayed as selfish, calculating, dangerous maniacs, against whose actions the society must be protected. Their scientific acumen is suspect and their science must be distrusted. Exaggeration reins. A chemistry lab is brewing a potential nuclear disaster and a genetic discovery leads to eugenics.

As medical knowledge grows constantly and changes rapidly, it is difficult to keep up with more than a portion of current information. The disease patterns in our society are changing. The demands on future health professionals reflect such changes in the needs of our diverse society. General attitudes toward science as an unmitigated danger are not very constructive.

Most of my peers are well-intentioned, vulnerable people with feelings. Some are endearingly awkward and naïve in their search of the ultimate truth, on the opposite end from the malevolent creatures of fiction. There is also a range of science, from the precise, orderly pursuits to the anarchy of serendipitous upheavals. There are mistakes and false starts. There are boring stretches to be endured while collecting data, between an exciting new hypothesis and the final attempt to organize an ungodly mess of facts within the boundaries of the theory currently in vogue. There are the lean early years of postdoc survival on the cutting edge of science, and the later frustration due to failure to secure coveted NIH grant funds. There is the incredible amount of information that one must be ready to digest continually in order to do science successfully. In short, scientists are human and science is a human pursuit, a job like any other. There is no typical scientist or one type of science.

Personal myopia and misuse of facts for the purpose of entertainment aside, our contemporary life demands a set of checks and balances on all matters, including those in science. My intention was not to issue a prescription on how to do "good" science, but to demystify those scientific complexities that I could by using a vocabulary that wasn't less precise but was more comprehensible, providing a close-up of science and helping create a better-informed consumer. But my articles did not sell and I had to look for other ways to support myself.

Soon after the magazine-writing fiasco, I found an ad in the paper for a part-time job as a receptionist to an obstetrician-gynecologist, who had an office near my apartment. The job interview was brief, establishing only my familiarity with computers and the days I would be available. I prudently withheld some crucial facts from my CV, such as the PhD degree and postdoctoral training in reproductive physiology, as well as my years as an academic. Idealizing my recent exposure to magazine writing, I told my new boss that I was a freelance medical writer trying to supplement my income with part-time employment.

To my surprise and delight, the doctor's office, which was run by his wife, was fully computerized. There were two nurses—a middle-aged mother of four and a younger single woman, who was studying epidemiology at night. It was a pleasant little group, and I was soon incorporated into it. It was also a very busy doctor's office, and extremely well organized. No patient ever waited more than ten minutes. The appointment schedules were printed a day in advance; the patients' medical charts were pulled the day before their appointments and placed next to my desk in alphabetical order. The nurses' and physician's notes were entered by computer. All billing was also computerized through a custom-designed program, a costly novelty at that time. The office had an ultrasound machine and other instruments, all linked and interfaced with the main computer. At my desk I had a computer terminal and a phone. I was expected to greet the patients, check their names and appointment times, usher them into a pleasantly decorated waiting room, and give their medical charts to one of the nurses. Phone calls were infrequent, because the appointment scheduling was computerized and done by the office manager. At the end of each appointment, I took care of billing, keeping the copayment and other checks in a locked drawer and entering the appropriate information into the computer.

My boss, the gynecologist, was a fair and competent clinician, respected and liked by his patients. He was superbly calm during any emergency, which arose frequently, since he was also an obstetrician. He was patient and understanding and always found time for any unscheduled patient. It never was a problem. His wife, the office manager, made time and room for everybody with a smile. She never complained about being too busy and dismissed most schedule changes as just one of those unpredictable but manageable problems of her husband's profession. I loved working there. Each day we had a short communal lunch, with takeout food ordered, delivered and paid for everybody.

My birthday fell on a workday after I had been an employee for only a few weeks. They surprised me with an after-hours birthday party, a cake, and presents. The manager gave me a beautiful blooming cactus plant that kept cheering up my apartment for months—long after I left that job.

I was paid commensurate with the information I had disclosed on my edited CV, but still well for a receptionist in a doctor's office. But it was a part-time job and I continued looking for a full-time job better suited to my qualifications. When I finally got it, it involved a long commute. Keeping the part-time receptionist's job was out of the question. I was sincerely sorry to leave this welcoming place. When I resigned, explaining the need for a full time job, they gave me a going-away party. Obliged to be honest to these nice people, I confessed to my doctored CV. The gynecologist just laughed it off, wished me luck, and said that he was sorry to lose such a terrific and knowledgeable receptionist. I suspected that he had suspected I had removed information from my CV, although he and his wife fully accepted the subterfuge and never accused me of deliberate deception.

"Alexandra," he said to me, "just imagine what a terrific anecdote I will have for my cocktail parties, when I tell them that my receptionist was a doctor."

While working for him, I was introduced to the clinical side of reproductive physiology, the practice of obstetrics and gynecology. I never suspected that my next career move would be partially in that direction, and that the months spent in his office would turn out to be a valuable apprenticeship for my next academic position. For each of his patients I had to follow their medical history; for the billing, I had to list the procedures and the final diagnosis. When I asked questions, he readily explained the pertinent details, occasionally going over test results and their significance, the sonograms and the physical exams, guiding me through the process of arriving at a diagnosis and treatment. On my part, I spent hours willingly learning the boring basics of the international coding system for diseases, the ICD-9, a system for coding medical procedures and diagnoses. This was an unexpected benefit and it became a fitting asset for the future supervisor of research of residents in obstetrics and gynecology, which, after years of life's intrusions, became my next job.

Six

My new job was an academic job at a medical center, supervising research and conducting journal clubs in the department of obstetrics and gynecology. My students were young doctors in residency training. I lectured and conducted individual meetings on research methodology, and led discussions about recent findings from clinical literature during journal club meetings.

The OB-GYN residents were a varied group, some with foreign medical degrees, some with degrees from US medical schools, but they shared many attitudes. One of the most perplexing was their avoidance of numbers. Their notes were always in some undecipherable and illogical medical shorthand. For some reason all nouns, especially in differential diagnoses, were capitalized and not always spelled correctly. Exhausted at the end of the day from their clinical obligations, they had little time or motivation for reading. My lectures and their meetings with me were definitely not high on their priority lists, but they reluctantly submitted because it was required.

After years of obtaining information from textbooks or

any kind of printed matter, they were eager for interaction with patients and hands-on clinical experience. The majority were ill prepared in basic sciences due to the recently revised medical school curriculum, which did not give them a sufficient foundation to build upon and truly practice evidence-based medicine. Their knowledge of statistics was, at best, rudimentary.

The attending physicians—their clinical supervisors—were just as busy and seldom found time for reading entire journal articles. Instead, they relied on abstracts and summaries without deeper analysis. Research investigation could not be further from the residents' minds, although officially their residency training curriculum required some inclusion of it. They could not graduate without fulfilling the research requirements. In theory, my job was to supervise their research progress, but in practice, it felt like dragging them by the hand each reluctant step by step. What I had to offer was of secondary importance, and our individual conferences had to be repeatedly rescheduled—often after I reminded them that they had missed yet another appointment with me. They were not allowed to turn off their pagers when in the hospital, so that our meetings, when they did occur, were interrupted by phone calls they had to make in order to answer beeper summons.

It was my intention initially to teach them the basics of scientific approach, since I was not so naïve as to expect all of them to produce a publishable piece of research during their residency. The unavoidable start of any research project is a formal research proposal. It has a clear and logical structure and is usually submitted to a variety of committees for review and approval. A clinical research proposal is evaluated on its scientific and clinical merit. It is a mandatory part of any request for research funds. The easiest part of it is the introduction, which is supposed to summarize findings from clinical literature in the proposed area of study. Yet it was the part residents invariably got wrong, in that they thought more was better and proceeded to describe the history of medicine in general, rather than concentrating on the salient points of previous research in the area they planned to investigate.

They were equally inept in specifying a clear objective of the study. This led to inefficient data collection and an inability to perform valid statistical analyses, yielding results without definitive conclusions. The most crucial and difficult part of any research proposal is its design, its methodology. Since the results are not yet available, a research proposal has to stand firmly on its methodological feet, so to speak, in order to be approved and ultimately funded.

Thus, in my opinion, the basic research requirement for all OB-GYN residents was to write a research proposal that could be submitted to the departmental and institutional committees for review and approval. In it they were required to list the reasons for the proposed study, state a clear objective, and describe a detailed methodology. Since they were physicians in training and eager to develop their clinical skills, I assumed most would propose studies involving patients. So I made it a requirement that they take the NIH online course in clinical research ethics, which included a certificate of completion. Ethics in research would seem to be a human necessity, and logic dictated that the patients' consent for any procedures should be obtained prior to the procedure. In their eagerness to collect data, clinical researchers often view the research consent form as a burdensome hurdle or even worse, a formality.

The federal regulations guiding clinical research require consent forms and actually specify what is to be included in them. It was undeniably one of my major responsibilities to teach the residents the fundamentals of research ethics. Evaluations, no matter who is doing them, are subjective. A certificate of completion of the NIH online ethics course freed me from any perceived subjectivity in evaluations and made the residents aware that their patients were not just objects of study, but people.

Each July, the beginning of the academic year in graduate medical training, I gave a set of introduction-to-research lectures for the incoming residents. At the end of their first year of specialty training, they were supposed to hand in their research proposals. That proved a bit optimistic on my part. The first year of any residency is essentially a year of clinical orientation. Residents are learning their way around the hospital: who is in charge of what; how to deal with the never-ending paperwork related to each patient; and how to take a patient's history quickly and present it to the attending physician, ready with arguments for an efficient diagnostic evaluation. Yes, they could have learned some of this as medical students, but somehow most of them had missed that opportunity.

Writing a research proposal was a chore that only a small number of them accomplished on the first try. The idea was that if they had a research proposal written in their first year, they could, if the proposal was approved, start collecting data in their second year. In the third year of their residency training, they could analyze the collected data and use the results for an abstract of the study. The abstracts could then be sent off for presentation at a professional conference. After the presentation, they would be in a position to write a manuscript for publication.

My description of the research curriculum was brilliant in theory and it all sounded great on paper. The OB-GYN chairman was delighted with my outline of resident research requirements and the steps leading toward research publications. Research publications were what everybody was after! Each resident shared me as a research advisor, but also needed a separate clinical advisor, which gave the attending physicians an easy way to conference presentations and publications. Research publications led to academic promotions and academic titles, which provided the attending physicians with excuses to curtail their time in the clinic. They loved me for providing them with this opportunity, especially since they seldom had to actually venture into any specific advising for the duration of the project. They had me to do the advising.

Journal clubs are a vehicle of dissemination of recently published medical information, the basis for the evidence in evidence-based medicine. As the residents were too busy and often too inexperienced to select valid clinical research articles for journal club discussion, and the attending physicians too busy with seeing patients, the responsibility of selecting the articles fell on me. That meant reading some twenty articles on a particular topic and selecting two to be discussed during the next monthly journal club. It also meant reviewing the selected article with the resident who would be presenting, since in their avoidance of numbers, tables, and graphs they seldom grasped the full implications of the data analysis and had a tendency to skip the results section of a research publication. It was my job to make them concentrate on that rather than on the discussion part, where the authors gave their reasons for not doing a better job in the first place.

Day in and day out I wondered anew at how few of the future medical specialists actually read an entire article published in a peer-reviewed medical journal and how many avoided graphs and tables and parroted the conclusions of the authors. Their aversion of critical thinking and analysis was rampant and infectious. The residents had to be discouraged from giving PowerPoint presentations of the articles in order to preserve the original rationale for a journal club: reading an article in full, followed by a critical appraisal of the findings and their relevance to clinical practice.

The journal clubs improved in quality with practice, and by the time the residents were in their third or fourth years, the discussions were increasingly more constructive. They even generated ideas for new research. I was inclined to believe that my meetings with them mattered.

The next journal club topic was human papilloma virus (HPV) infection—my old friend from my Caracas days. To diagnose HPV infection, a simple Pap smear was not sufficient. A considerable number of research studies argued for additional tests for the Pap smear. Articles about viral oncogenicity had just started to be published. A persistent HPV infection was being implicated as a necessary but not sufficient cause of cervical cancer. Not all types of the virus are equally virulent. There are about a hundred different types and only about half of them infect the genital areas. HPV infections are common in young women, but most of those infections resolve themselves spontaneously over a period of time. The prevalence among sexually active women depends on age and the population risk. A proportion of infections will lead to cervical lesions with mild dysplasia, but if the infection persists, the lesions might progress and pose a risk of cervical cancer.

I had chosen two articles to be discussed at the next journal club. One of the articles investigated age as a factor in HPV infection. The other offered valid evidence associating promiscuity in gay men with persistent HPV infections with HPV types similar to those that were believed to lead to cervical cancer in women.

The identification of molecular markers related to HPV infection and HPV vaccines were things of the future. Many gynecologists still resisted the idea of a virus causing cancer, and even more resisted the idea of modifying the scoring of Pap tests. This journal club was clinically challenging in respect to the idea of HPV oncogenicity, and I wanted to make sure that the residents scheduled to present the articles understood the results and their potential implications for clinical practice.

It proved to be a difficult journal club. It deteriorated into a shouting match with sharp and loud arguments. Eventually the consensus of the clinicians at the meeting was that it might be of interest to include HPV testing as part of Pap smears, despite the additional cost. Not all were convinced, and many advocated waiting for more definitive studies linking the virus to cervical cancer.

The topic of the journal club also disturbed me personally. When I went home, I thought about my own history. I thought about the time in Venezuela when my first cervical lesions were diagnosed and the need for a hysterectomy. The time when life stopped. The time when I learned that Will was not my future. The time when I had been forced to accept that I could not have more children. How I regretted the decision to have the abortion!

If the problems that eventually led to my hysterectomy were due to a silent, subclinical, undiagnosed HPV infection, how did I get it? I was not promiscuous. I was pretty sure Carlos was not promiscuous; he was hardly interested in sex. Was it Will? Was Will promiscuous? Was Will ... gay?

The harder I tried to remember, the more events came to mind supporting this idea. I was not sure what hurt more, the realization that I had been in love with a gay man or that I felt so completely a woman while in love with a gay man. All of my doubts about my personal identity surfaced again, making me miserable. Suddenly the information about HPV became all important. I started reading all the articles I could get my hands on. Many articles gave solid evidence of the link between promiscuity in gay men and HPV infection. I reviewed my dissertation and thought up studies to explore the issues to a greater depth.

One of the female OB-GYN residents, Jenny, became intrigued by the association of HPV infection and age. She wrote an excellent research proposal to do a retrospective study on a sample of three hundred patients. The study was approved by the departmental research committee and the institutional review board. The results of the study unequivocally showed that the proportion of sexually active girls infected with HPV at the ages of twelve to fourteen was higher than the proportion of sexually active women at the age of thirty and older. The difference was statistically significant, with little probability that the findings were due to chance. Jenny collected all the information and I helped her organize and analyze data. The abstract of the study was submitted for presentation at the next annual GYN Society meeting. Jenny kept coming to my office weekly asking if I thought the abstract would be accepted. "Maybe", she said, "we should have waited for a larger sample."

"I think, Jenny," I answered, "you should not second-guess yourself and just wait for the decision concerning your abstract."

When the abstract was accepted as an oral platform presentation, part of the panel on HPV infections in gynecology, she was ecstatic.

We made slides together, playing with graphic features to make the most effective 3-D and color graphs. We debated each sentence and each phrase in the text, changing them time after time until the passage felt just right. Finally the slides were done; the presentation was ready.

Jenny came to my office on a daily basis now, often in her green scrubs after surgeries. She was a third-year resident and was proud to be already doing hysterectomies. None of the other residents in the program had had their research accepted for an annual clinical meeting. This was a first. Jenny was excited, bursting with pride one day and full of doubts the next. I shared her pride and enthusiasm, and also some of her doubts. I remembered the disappointment I had felt after one of my early oral presentations at an international meeting generated not a single question from the audience. But I also remembered the feeling of accomplishment when a well-known scientist stopped by my poster at another meeting and kept asking questions, discussing my findings.

Jenny also wanted to know what the regulation attire was for a presentation at an annual professional meeting.

She had never attended one. Residents were seldom sent to national meetings. Was it appropriate to wear a pantsuit? The common attire for residents who went on interviews seeking fellowship positions at that time was a navy-blue suit, pumps with a medium heel, a white blouse, and a strand of pearls—for women, of course. Men were supposed to wear dark suits, pale shirts, subdued ties, and polished shoes. With a substantial dose of chagrin, I remembered the letter I received as a postdoc in Caracas from the dean of the medical school, informing me to wear a suit and a tie to the orientation meeting. I arrived early with one of Carlos's ties in the pocket of my pantsuit and asked the dean—who was drinking coffee and pleasantly chatting with some new postdocs and residents—whether I really was expected to wear a tie and if I should put it on, since I had brought one with me. Needless to say the dean was not amused. He remembered my name for the rest of my postdoc period and, although I could never prove it, rejected my requisitions for research supplies without fail. Eventually I learned to ask a male postdoc to add my requisitions to his and got them approved each time.

I assured Jenny that she could wear anything she wanted, even her hair loose. She didn't. She gave an excellent presentation, dressed in a tailored navy-blue suit, a white silk blouse, a strand of pearls, and her beautiful long hair pinned up.

I sat in the front row where she could see me, to provide support. There were numerous questions after her presentation, and a lively discussion about the role of age in HPV infections followed. Jenny's presentation was an unmitigated success.

I stayed for the rest of the meeting, but Jenny flew home

after her presentation. She had rounds the next day, and the institutional funds for her stay at the meeting were limited to two days. But she was so buoyant with the experience at her first annual national meeting she probably could have cashed in her airline ticket and floated back home on her pride.

Jenny worked hard on her manuscript in her last year of residency. We had numerous consultations and there was a lot of rewriting and editing. Finally the manuscript was ready. The chairman of the department and her clinical advisors, both of whom were included as authors, read it and approved. It was sent for publication to the "green" journal.

Obstetrics and gynecology had many peer-reviewed journals, but two in particular were considered prestigious. Both were published by the national OB-GYN societies, one with a gray jacket and the other with a green jacket. The "gray" journal had a custom of publishing research work by residents once a year. The "green" journal did not separate contributions by the author's year of training. We missed the deadline for the resident issue of the "gray" journal and sent the manuscript to the "green" journal. The manuscript, however, was rejected. The rejection letter essentially said that since the first author, Jenny, was still in residency training, the study was inappropriate for publication. When she finished her fellowship training—or better yet, started practicing gynecology—she should try again. The letter also failed to include any specific criticisms, a customary practice for research manuscripts submitted for publication.

There was no way to console Jenny. She actually cried in my office. I offered to help her rewrite the manuscript and to send it to another journal. I tried to convince her that her research findings were worth publishing, but she was crushed beyond repair. And although we had previously discussed her potential participation in clinical research, she was adamant that there would be no research in her future. Years later Jenny has gained prominence as a gynecologic laparoscopic surgeon and is a clinical professor at a medical school. But I wonder whether she would have contributed equally to clinical research were it not for an arbitrary, unfair decision by the "green" journal editors to reject her manuscript purely on the basis that it was written while she was still in residency training.

From then on I advised all residents with manuscripts worth publishing never to divulge their "still in training" status when submitting them for publication. The subterfuge—perhaps not the right word for it—worked on many future occasions, resulting in numerous publications.

The topic of HPV infections got me thinking again about Will. I began following events in Hollywood and read all I could, any article that mentioned his name or his movies. There were a fair number of them, some very successful. He had made them when I was in graduate school and during my postdoc years in Caracas. I thought I saw him in a photograph at a gay pride demonstration in San Francisco. None of the articles mentioned whether he was married. Too busy with work, I seldom went to the movies. I was not politically active and was certainly not gay. For many years I had been too busy raising Jason. And now I was too busy to investigate further precise events in my past.

The present was busy and in itself absorbing. The

past was past; painful and done with. Will did not love me. He had never attempted to get in touch. He had not wanted me in his life. Our life together had been just an illusion, a costly illusion, whose dues I already had paid in full. Perhaps Will indeed preferred men. The sadness of rejection turned into despair of betrayal. It still hurt to think about the past, but I was glad that the discomfort was no longer as acute. And it was easy to rationalize: if Will was gay, a life with him would not have been a happy life. I refused to further speculate on the details. The past intruded, but the present incorporated the intrusions as minor upheavals, easily smoothed out, easily denied. It seemed futile to seek further evidence of Will's love life. I had no desire to know the details. Trying to be realistic about events, I concentrated on my work, on the tasks at hand.

In Caracas, I was convinced that having to take care of Jason kept me sane. Kept me from completely falling apart and, perhaps, attempting suicide. Jason gave me reasons to live. There was this innocent little person who needed me and depended on me. Parental responsibility rescued me. Later, the parental responsibility became an easy burden as Jason grew into a confident, accomplished young man, a loving husband, and then a father.

My identity kept slowly evolving, from an adolescent girl, who at the threshold of her emerging sexuality, cherished tender kisses in the time of blooming cyclamen; to a married woman—a mother—who thought she had lost her sex appeal; to a woman who regained her sexuality when in love with a gay man; to a busy professional. A painfully long journey of discovery through pitfalls, depression, hard work, and the effort to survive from day to day. This candid retrospective analysis left me satisfied with the outcome. I felt less fractured, mended.

Reading and research in clinical obstetrics and gynecology gave me an opportunity to obtain a separate insight into being a woman and a mother. The insight was more extensive and more objective than what a woman normally acquires by giving birth. In addition to that personal knowledge, I could pursue a scholarly investigation into motherhood and womanhood. As if my studies in reproductive physiology were given meaning. Detached from immediate reality, the experimental studies on ewes always felt slightly superfluous to the understanding of what it is to be a mother and a woman. And my personal experience as a mother to Jason was separate from the ewes as mothers. Now, through reading, journal clubs, case reports, and research in obstetrics and gynecology, I was gaining new knowledge about universal motherhood, and universal womanhood. It was no longer an abstract intellectual pursuit of the causes of infection and its role in premature labor, or a personal feeling. It was also finding the best treatment for a mother in preterm labor, a mother about to lose her twins, a woman with a uterus invaded by fibroids who was about to lose the chance of ever being a mother. Real people suffered, real people's lives were damaged. There was a real need to help them, to solve an immediate problem ... and to rejoice at a birth after initial difficulties.

Each residency in a medical center is accredited through annual reviews by the graduate medical education committees and their respective national professional societies, which dictate the curriculum of training and encourage a variety of research-related activities. As the director of research for the department of obstetrics and gynecology, I considered it reasonable to consult other directors of research that supervised residents in emergency medicine, internal medicine, pediatrics, surgery, and radiology. I wanted to learn how other clinical departments were dealing with research requirements for their residents.

My counterpart in surgery was another woman PhD, Dr. Esther Villanova, who seemed pleased to meet me but stressed her independence from others. To my surprise she knew little about ethics legislation in clinical research and said that compliance with federal regulations in that respect had never been an issue at our institution. When I asked about research consent forms, she asked me what they were. As I began to explain, she seemed bored, probably not wanting to be burdened with such apparently trivial issues. She was an attractive woman, with fashionably styled blonde hair, meticulously made up. Shorter than average, she wore high heels. Most women in direct contact with patients avoided high heels. Esther was also ostentatiously garbed in expensive clothing, but what I envied most was her large office with an up-to-date computer and a statistical software package that my department had yet to purchase for me. She was separated from her husband, a surgeon. It was rumored that her divorce settlement would include at the very least her red Mercedes coupe and a three-bedroom condominium in Manhattan, as well as a six-figure annual alimony.

She was not much help, although we had a pleasant meeting. We did not discuss our research responsibilities in great detail, but talked instead about local events, cafeteria food, fashion, and children, although she did not have any.

A few years later I learned that she went through infertility treatments with her new husband and had twin sons.

My counterpart in radiology was an older man whose son was one of the attending physicians in the hospital. He offered me a cup of Turkish coffee. Or perhaps it was Lebanese, since he told me about his life as a medical student in Lebanon and why he immigrated to the States. He never took the medical board exams and could not practice medicine, but he was enormously proud of his son and daughter, both of whom were physicians. He was of a slight build and agile for his age, which I guessed to be in midseventies. His eyes were dark brown with a direct, slightly impertinent gaze. He smiled a lot and occasionally touched his slim moustache with his fingers, sort of pressing it into shape. We chatted effortlessly. He did know about federal ethics regulations in clinical research and showed me documentation of the research reviews in his department. An impressive number of national clinical trials in oncology had been funded by the NCI, the National Cancer Institute. I asked whether any residents in radiology were involved in this substantial research.

He shook his head. "No! Oh, no. No residents are involved unless they happened to be rotating through the unit and can then observe. As you know, clinical trials funded by NCI have rigorously reviewed protocols that our hospital must follow without alterations or we would lose the funding."

Yes, I knew about the mandatory reviews of clinical research protocols and also about the consent forms that each patient had to sign before volunteering for the trials.

"Is there an IRB here?" I asked, referring to an institutional review board, mandated by the federal government for all institutions conducting clinical research.

"There is a research committee, but not an IRB," he explained. "Our consent forms must, of course, be approved by this committee, but are generally not changed in any way."

"So what does the committee review?"

"Mostly the potential conflicts with the hospital's legal counsel."

I asked who chaired the research committee and he gave me the name of an eminent cardiologist, originally from India. Hoping that he would be able to clarify the resident research requirements and their involvement in clinical research, I made an appointment with his secretary to see him.

His secretary kept calling me and rescheduling our meeting, and finally asked whether my chairman had agreed to the meeting. I failed to understand why my chairman needed to know, but asked him nevertheless. I explained that in my role as director of research I would be attending research committee meetings, so it seemed logical to introduce myself as supervisor of resident research to the chair of the research committee. My chairman was busy at the time and said, yes, he approved the meeting, but had no time to discuss any details.

At the appointed hour I went to see the cardiologist and was ushered by his secretary into a large office with an imposing mahogany desk sitting on unexpectedly brilliant teal carpeting. One wall was covered in bookshelves with volumes of bound journals about internal medicine, surgery, and cardiology. The desk had no computer. It did have an expensive slide projector, two phones, and was covered with paperwork. I recognized patient medical record folders, the yellow oversized envelopes that contained X-ray films, journals opened one on top of another, a thick cardiology textbook. The research committee chairman was talking on the phone with his back to me. He eventually turned around and gestured for me to sit in one of the chairs in front of his desk.

Finally he ended his call. "Sit down, please, sit down, Mrs. ..."

I sat down. "Doctor..., sir." I corrected him in a soft voice, but distinctly.

"Oh, yes, a PhD. I am very busy as you can see. What is it that you want?"

"Well, since one of my responsibilities here is to supervise research of OB-GYN residents, I would like to know what is required in order to get their projects reviewed and approved. And, yes, I would like the schedule for the research committee meetings."

"A resident cannot be a PI—that is, a Principal Investigator—of any study. They need a clinician, an attending physician as a PI, and the research proposals are reviewed by the committee a month after they are submitted. Why exactly would you need the schedule of the meetings? Your chairman was given a copy in July."

"As I will be actively involved in resident research as well as teaching the residents research methodology, might I not be considered a PI at least on some of their projects? And I would like my own copy of the schedule of the meetings, since I will be attending them."

"Attending them? The research committee meetings? You plan to attend the meetings? Why? We already have a member of the committee for OB-GYN department.

You need not come. Besides since you don't have an MD degree, you cannot be a member of the medical board of this hospital, a requirement for a PI of a clinical study."

"I understand that Dr. Villanova has been attending your meetings regularly."

"Dr. Villanova?"

"Yes, she supervises research of residents in surgery."

"My dear, Mrs.— My dear ..." He looked at me in consternation, not sure of how to address me. "Esther comes to the meetings because she is an affiliate of the medical board. She is also a clinical psychologist, a pain specialist. She sees patients and charges for the service. We had no choice but to make her an affiliate of the medical board. An affiliate, not a member. But you are mistaken. Esther does not supervise research of residents, she does statistics for them. She analyzes data. She is at the meetings, yes, but she does not vote. Only full members of the medical board can be members of any hospital committees with voting privileges. If you insist on coming, your chairman will have to approve. But still, even if you attend the meetings he will need to select an attending physician from your department who can vote."

"What is the use of my coming to the meetings if I cannot vote?"

"We review a lot of clinical trials at this hospital whose protocols involve a fair amount of medical knowledge. How could we justify your voting since you do not have an MD? You are not qualified."

The meeting, obviously, did not go well. That I had a doctoral degree that had required a research dissertation and that I was an author of several research publications did not seem relevant for attending research committee meetings with voting privileges. I felt humiliated and remembered a cartoon from an old issue of the *Chronicle of Higher Education.* A recent PhD comes to a counter with a sign that says Terminal Degrees and offers his PhD diploma to the guy at the counter, saying, "I'd like to exchange my degree. It's not working for me."

That's exactly how I felt. My degree was not working for me. Perhaps I should have stayed in journalism. Perhaps ... But such thoughts brought about memories of Will. Well versed in this exercise, I pushed them away, out of my consciousness. No, I would not have been better off in journalism. I was going to make the degree in reproductive physiology work for me.

The OB-GYN chairman reluctantly approved my attendance of the monthly research committee meetings. I made it a point to always be on time and ready with pertinent questions about any of the studies under review. Esther attended the meetings too in her elegant, high-heeled attire, an ingratiating smile on her perfectly made-up face, entering just a bit late so that she would be noticed.

I kept my wardrobe fashionable yet professional, appearing at the meetings in suits and silk blouses, some jewelry, and freshly manicured nails. The jewelry bit was not too difficult, because Carlos had been generous with gold and silver earrings, pins and bracelets. And Jason once gave me a gorgeous silver necklace for one of my birthdays, and a gold ruby broach for another. I cherished any opportunity to wear them. And, actually, somewhat guiltily, I looked forward to these meetings as special occasions to parade in fashionable clothes and well groomed, in sharp contrast to white-lab-coated predominantly male attendees with their more appropriate terminal degrees. After years of working in research labs, clothed in jeans and T-shirts, this was a welcome change. I was proud to show that I was a woman. Furthermore, a woman who paid attention to her appearance and wished to be judged attractive. A smart, attractive woman professional.

Pleasure in my well-groomed appearance never distracted me from asking relevant questions. The chairman of the committee waited until the last possible moment to allow me to ask questions. In the beginning he was visibly surprised by their relevancy, and as the time progressed more and more annoyed, as if he wished he could prove that I had no right to be there, since I lacked the requisite MD degree. Other attending physicians often welcomed my questions. I asked them primarily to clarify important issues. Encouraged by their response, I soon felt confident enough to point out errors in research design and suggested methodological improvements.

Esther did her best to turn the research committee meetings into an intellectual battleground. Invariably she asked a question right after mine, as if to show that she too was well informed and knowledgeable and was not any less educated than I. It amused me, because her clinical psychology training, although strong on research design and statistical analysis, did not prepare her fully for most of the clinical research under review at those meetings. Reproductive physiology, my specialty, involved a fair amount of scientific background, and the clinical challenges, especially in obstetrics and gynecology, were a natural extension of the basic science inquiries. I read a lot of clinical literature for the journal clubs and it was relatively easy for me to understand most of the projects under review.

As the director of research I had no clinical responsibilities and did not see patients. I had the time to be conscientious about reading scientific and clinical literature, the luxury busy practicing clinicians did not always have.

Working at a medical center afforded me more than a rare glance into the practice of medicine, and with time I came to truly appreciate the hard work of most clinicians. Almost every day they made important decisions, life decisions. As obstetric and gynecologic surgeons, they held the scalpel, delivered the babies, held life in their hands.

Once during a discussion of indicators for Cesarean sections for an upcoming journal club, a resident jokingly asked me if I'd ever seen a C-section. I had to admit that I had not.

"Would you like to?"

I pondered whether I really would or would not and decided that it was safe to say yes. In my office, far away from the operating rooms and patient floors, there was only a slim probability of my ever being exposed to a C-section. I was wrong. The resident, a charming, confident young man of Italian descent, took me at my word and said he would be happy to arrange it.

"I will call you, put you in the yellow bunny suit, and show you the fastest C-section in this department. Under six minutes!"

"You must be joking," I said. "Under six minutes? Impossible!"

"No, that's my average," he bragged. "But you know I am not counting my first year. I was much slower then."

"You did C-sections in your first year?"

"Sure, everybody does in this residency. This residency

is good if you like to cut. So, Doc, what do you say? Can I call you for my next C-section?"

"Sure. Sure." I was far from sure, but was not going to admit it.

In a couple of days, while I was entering data into my computer and a little bored, sneaking a look out the window, happy that I had a window, I got a call to come down to L&D—the labor and delivery floor—because Dr. Caruso was about to perform a Cesarean and requested my presence. I have no idea how he accomplished that, because strictly speaking, I was not allowed there. Suddenly curious, I hurried to the elevators, kept pushing the buttons to speed up the journey, and there I was, in L&D.

I saw two other residents I recognized, one an OB-GYN resident and the other a pediatric resident. The OB-GYN resident brought me fresh scrubs, a yellow bunny suit, that covered me from head to toe, handed me a surgeon's mask, and pointed the way into the next room. The father of the baby was in there, holding his pregnant wife's hand and a video camera, along with a couple of nurses and Dr. Caruso.

"I'm so glad you could make it, Doc," he said to me. "Here we go."

Thus I witnessed a C-section. The first cuts and the blood did not bother me. I had seen some of that with the pregnant ewes in the Caracas lab. But I was astonished by the strength that was needed to pull apart the uterine tissue in order to extract the baby. The procedure was a success and done, yes, in about six minutes. I stayed until the last staple was applied. The baby boy was given Apgar scores of 9/9/9 after zero, five, and ten minutes of his life. I congratulated Dr. Caruso on his performance and could hear the newborn wailing as I walked toward the elevators. Such an uplifting, happy sound.

Back in my office, I tried to suppress a giggle that spontaneously sneaked out. I felt satisfaction mixed with pride that I had witnessed such an important event. An everyday event for Dr. Caruso, who still in training performed up to six such surgeries in a day, while I sat at the computer entering and analyzing data and reading clinical literature, feeling sort of important. It was the MDs who did important things. We PhDs, the basic science professionals, piled unnecessary importance onto what we did. I suddenly had greater respect for the medical profession and was proud to be part of the echelon of people who educated future physicians. Ludicrous as it sounded, I wanted to be as good in my job as humanly possible, to help in this business of healing and bringing about new life. I had a huge responsibility as a teacher, I realized, and I should never do anything half-heartedly, regardless of the alleged shortcomings of my terminal degree.

It took time for the vestiges of my Caracas years to melt away and disappear. The second-guessing of myself, the indecision, the self-loathing, and depression were in the past, receding into oblivion. I was well into the process of recovering my lost identities, that of a confident and accomplished woman and active professional. I allowed myself an analysis of the more than ten years it had taken to purge Will out of my life. I calmly examined the aftermath of my disastrous love, passionate and blinding, devastating and doomed. Carlos's indifference and Will's rejection were irrelevant. I did not need their love or approval to be a woman of substance, a person. I did not need the eminent cardiologist to doubt or approve my medical science acumen. I had full confidence in what I was doing, recognizing its educational importance, proud to be allowed to participate. Though my effort might not be fully appreciated, it contributed to something worthwhile. I believed in its value and did not need external approvals. I approved. That was all I needed! I was healed. It had taken time, but I liked my new confident persona. Perhaps love was not essential. Professional success was restorative. It healed and reconciled.

Epilogue

Crei mi hogar apagado
y revolví la ceniza ...
Me quemé la mano.

—Antonio Machado, *Proverbio y cantares, LVIII*

I REREAD THE LETTERS. Again. And again...The paper of some was yellowed and fragile, moist and stained with my tears in others. A few were neatly tucked in their envelopes, others naked, just there, uncovered. Some had been hastily written on lined paper, while others showed deliberate intent, carefully dated in the right hand corners. They were all tender, immediate. I could hear Will's voice saying those lovely words as I read them. The voice formed a soft embrace around my shoulders. I felt protected, encapsulated in love. I truly had been loved by this man who wrote the letters. It was true: Will had loved me. I kept reading the letters over and over to keep this precious feeling alive. Slowly and deliberately, the unacknowledged resentment that had lain buried in the depths of my inner self began rising to the surface in infinitesimally small steps. It spilled over the edges, gliding ever so slowly—this slime of resentment—out of my soul. As it inched out, freeing me of years of imprisonment, my spirits lifted. Newly liberated, newly redeemed, I was willing to forgive Will for the past rejection, for the change in him. It was not that I wanted him back or wanted to become a couple again at this late date. I just wished I could tell him that I no longer hated those frozen years. Past was past. No use reliving the betrayal, or the doubts, or the multitude of other similar feelings, even if in his mind there was nothing to be forgiven for, nothing to atone ...

I wanted him to know that I cherished the letters and believed them and did not mind that they were no longer current. Life had changed us. Circumstances had changed. We had loved each other in the past. There had been times when I was hurt, angry and confused. And a time when I had tried to understand why he had left me, why he did not wait for me, why he did not fight for me.

When Carlos found the letters, they were an instrument of pain and suffering. When they vanished I kept wishing I had them to assure myself that I mattered to this one person, that he loved the woman in me. When doubts arose about his masculinity—and, in turn, my femininity—I doubted there ever had been proof of our love. A friend once told me that love is fluid. That many people love both men and women with equal intention. I could not accept that then. I could not comprehend bisexuality. If Will was gay, how could he have loved me, a woman? Or if he did love me, what exactly did he see in me?

The relationship with Carlos never gave better answers to my anxious introspective probing, my meditation on the questions of identity, the true nature of my persona. It was becoming clear to me that it was possible Will had loved me. I slowly allowed this idea to grow. I squeezed it against my heart with a fearful force as if not to lose it again, not to enter the labyrinthine paths of doubt. I struggled to nestle within his thoughts and feelings, smoothing the edginess of painful memories, allowing the warmth and joy to emerge.

And then, suddenly, I had the urge to see Will, talk to him, and tell him that I forgave him for the years of worries, uncertainties, and suspicions. Even if he no longer wished to acknowledge our troubled history, I had the desire to beg him to accept the past and to bring it into the present. We merge the past with the present all the time. The past lives within us in our memories, sometimes corrupted, sometimes true, sometimes at the periphery of daily existence, sometimes at its very core. So I wished our past to be recognized as having rights to reside in my present as well and, perhaps in some form, in the future.

How did I find Will? Over the years his name had become known as his films, often controversial, collected both praise and criticism and a couple of Oscar nominations. Although he had a website, it was not so easy to locate his home address. He worked in Hollywood, and once someone mentioned that he lived in Burbank. But there were so many communities. How did I find out? I called some of the people from the university days to ask whether they had kept in touch with Will, but lost the courage to explain why I wanted to find him and learned nothing of use.

Days went by. Daily tasks took charge of the passing time. I had stored the letters in a box I had found in a stationary store. The box was blue with purple circles and green abstractly intersecting waves. It looked like a small sarcophagus with a gently curved top. A perfect little tomb for love letters. A perfect tomb for a love rejected, a love acknowledged, a love that no longer mattered. I placed the box with the letters on my desk to be readily observed, not obscured, and not hidden – in plain view and in touch with the surroundings to become an integral part of my present ordinary life. A part of the present with its acknowledged existence.

Even the most well-intentioned plans do not succeed. It was difficult to locate Will, probably because somewhat hesitant, I did not try very hard. Then one evening I thought I heard his name mentioned on the evening news. The newscaster was saying that Will had been admitted to a Los Angeles hospital for pneumonia. A PR person came on and repeated what the newscaster had already said. Will's two best-known films were also mentioned, scenes shown ... Other news came on and there was no more talk of Will. But now I knew where to find him.

Pneumonia? Well, I thought, he would have to stay in the hospital for a few days. It might give me an opportunity to see him under relatively acceptable circumstances. Yes, I would go to Los Angeles and visit him in the hospital—bring some flowers ... and the letters.

I called the airlines and made the reservations. And then I looked in the mirror. Would Will recognize me? A widow. Some twenty pounds heavier. Short white hair instead of the dark waves of my youth. I hoped the eyes were the same. But no, not really. The corners showed wrinkles. Wrinkles? They populated my face as if born there. Of course it was I in the reflection, but an *I* Will has never seen. I bemoaned being so old. It usually did not bother me, but now? Would this wrinkled face scare Will out of recognition?

Aged or not, sensitive about it or not, it was me now. No use trying to wish for the impossible. I smiled at my image. At least the teeth looked fine and smiling improved my reflection. I smiled at my image again and started talking to it.

"Hello, Will. I heard you were sick and decided to come and visit you."

What the ... What was I thinking? Was this trip a good idea? Had the letters made me foolishly spontaneous? Had briefly resurrected love destroyed all common sense and a modicum of caution?

But the plane ticket was bought, and at my age being embarrassed or unsure of my actions and behavior was silly. I pulled out the small black suitcase I used for overnight trips and started packing. I packed my best two suits and several silk blouses, a favorite sweater, a pair of comfortable shoes, a few scarves, because I could not decide which one looked best. I decided against the brown suit and packed black pants and a lime-green jacket. I loved that jacket and wore it to special occasions and dinners at good restaurants. Then, as an afterthought, I packed my black suit. It was an expensive suit. Well, expensive for me. When I bought it, it had been more than I could afford, but looked elegant and I received compliments when I wore it. One cannot always trust compliments, but I was ready to be optimistic about my appearance. I could choose clothes, but could not remove the wrinkles around my eyes or grow my hair long overnight.

The additional benefit of my black suit was that it almost

did not wrinkle—unlike my skin. And I could wear any color blouse with it, including black. But no, a black blouse would look too depressing. I packed a pale rose-colored blouse and then added a black blouse to wear underneath the green jacket and with the black trousers. I closed the suitcase in hope that when closed it would not generate a need to be repacked again.

But I almost forgot the letters. I grabbed the little sarcophagus and stuffed it in the bag as well. Finally I added some toiletries and make-up. I wore very little make-up when young, but still, much more than now. Eyeliner, yes, mascara, no. A couple of different shades of lipstick. Lipstick was always a problem. I had to pack several, because I usually decided at the last moment on which one. Ready. I took a shower and washed my hair, went to bed, and set the alarm.

The next morning I made myself a nice breakfast and took a cab to the airport. The flight seemed endless but was otherwise uneventful. I watched the movie so I would not have to think of Will, the hospital, and the nature of my visit. It did not work completely. The decision about the trip seemed spontaneous, but I knew it had not been all that spontaneous. Ever since Jason gave me the letters, Will had been constantly on my mind.

We landed and I took a cab, instructing the driver to leave me at a hotel in the vicinity of the hospital. The taxi driver was extremely helpful when I mentioned the nature of my visit and that I had flown from New York to visit an old sick friend.

The hotel was of a medium size and had a cheerfully decorated lobby. I got a room despite not having a reservation and went up to freshen up after the long flight.

I was tired and hungry. Although my intention had been to go to the hospital immediately, I was just too tired. I ordered dinner from room service and, feeling luxurious, asked for a bottle of merlot with it. I took a shower and fell asleep. The next morning, after a room-service breakfast, I put on my lime-green jacket, black pants and shirt, and a cheerful scarf. Looking in the mirror, I decided I looked presentable and sufficiently elegant, regardless of my age, or maybe despite it. The hotel had a flower shop and I bought some red tulips.

The ride to the hospital was short. At the information desk I asked the receptionist for directions to Will's room. The receptionist was a respectful young woman with a beautiful tan. Her name tag said, Carole.

She checked her computer and said they did not have a patient by that name.

"I heard on the news on television that he was hospitalized with pneumonia a couple of days ago," I explained. "I flew from New York to see him. We are old friends," I added.

Carole looked uncertain for a moment. Then, apparently registering the impatience and worry on my face, decided to go against the rules of patient confidentiality. "Oh, wait a minute," she said. "Yes, yes, I remember. Yes, indeed, I recognize the name now. Yes, he was admitted two days ago. Let me check again." She looked at her computer screen and said, "I don't see the room number. Just a second. Let me check the discharge lists."

I stood waiting, my disappointment mixed with anxiety about this uncharacteristic gesture of mine, this spontaneous trip to nowhere, growing.

Carole typed and looked at the computer screen, typed

some more and looked at the computer screen. Finally, she looked at me and said, "I think you should go to the third floor and ask for Dr. Graham. He might be able to help locate the patient for you."

Thanking Carole, I went to look for the elevator to the third floor. The hospital lobby was huge and very busy with many people jostling one another in a hurry to get to the right place. It took me awhile to locate the right bank of elevators. The elevator arrived, opened its automatic doors, and I entered with a large group of people. Eventually it chimed on the third floor. I got out, located the nurses' station, and asked for Dr. Graham.

A male nurse was expecting me, saying that Carole had called and Dr. Graham would see me shortly. He directed me to a waiting room. There were chairs but I remained standing, looking at the signs on the walls, surprised to see Isolation and Infection Wing. Was Will's pneumonia more fulminant?

Dr. Graham was a tall, balding man in his fifties, who looked at me through his rimless glasses with concern and undisguised curiosity. He shook my hand and introduced himself. His manner was polite and pleasant, but obviously of a very busy physician. He escorted me to an office furnished in light-colored wood. The desk was buried under papers. He gestured toward one of the two chairs in front of it and then noticed some journals on it. He took them away and apologized for the mess. The skin of his hands, I noticed, was whitish and dry, as if he kept washing and drying them repeatedly. He probably kept them powdered under the plastic gloves too long.

"Are you a relative?" he asked as we both sat. "Carole said you came from New York to see Will."

"No, not a relative. A friend. An old friend. Will was my teacher. I studied journalism."

"Are you from the press?" he asked, visibly annoyed.

"No, no, no. My journalism studies were interrupted. I never finished. I later studied physiology...this is not important. ..Will was one of my favorite teachers. He was an excellent teacher. We were close friends. Very close friends. This was in New York before he went to Hollywood and became famous." I was nervously mumbling, looking for words that would explain this increasingly haphazard visit of mine.

"I see." The disconcerted look that had appeared on his face when I mentioned journalism vanished. Now he looked at me with a gentle sadness, apparently having made the decision to be frank.

"I am afraid I have some bad news."

"Is Will in intensive care?"

"No. Not anymore. He died last night, around midnight. Peacefully." He paused, seeing the consternation on my face, and added gently, "I am so sorry."

I was speechless. I looked at him, not comprehending.

"I am sorry for your loss. Truly sorry ..."

The information stayed outside and did not penetrate. I did not understand. Dr. Graham sensed how upsetting the news was. In order to ease my bewilderment and distress, he offered an explanation.

"This was not Will's first visit. During the last year he was here many times. His condition deteriorated drastically within the last eight months."

"His condition? I did not know that he was ill."

"Will had AIDS. The medication had stopped working. His immunity was drastically compromised. I am sorry we could not help him anymore. It is sad. He was a very talented man. He must have been a hell of a teacher! I am so sorry."

"I didn't know. I had no idea," I kept murmuring. "I brought tulips."

"Yes, I can see. How lovely. He would have liked that."

"Did you know him well, Dr. Graham?"

"Yes, rather. He had been my patient for years. One of my favorite patients. But there was very little hope this time. I knew we could not help him. I am sorry."

We both remained silent for a while, and then Dr. Graham said, "If you would like to stay here for a while, please do so. Regrettably, I have to see a patient in crisis. When Carole called about a friend of Will's who traveled from New York to see him, I made myself available, but I am sorry, I really must go now."

"Thank you, Dr. Graham. I should go ..."

I left the tulips at the nurses' station and asked whether they knew about funeral arrangements. They believed that Will's family wished for him to be cremated and that there would be a memorial service. They gave me the information, which I mechanically wrote on a piece of paper. So he was not going to be buried in a grave. I couldn't leave the letters, the box to be buried with him.

I did go to the memorial but stayed hidden in the crowd. It was not difficult. There were a lot of people, more than could be seated. Many people talked about him, but I daydreamed, crushed that I could not tell him that the letters were safe and that our love was safe, sheltered, and protected—that I meant to unite the past and the present.

I was surprised to see his large family seated in the

first few rows. He seldom talked about them. The two men, older versions of Will as I remembered him, must have been his brothers; the women with them, their wives. They were surrounded by several grown-up children and numerous grandchildren. There was an ancient woman in a wheelchair, wearing a hat with a veil that covered her eyes, crying and clenching a handkerchief in her trembling hands—probably his aunt. Sitting beside her were several middle-aged women. The women, I assumed, were his cousins.

I lacked the motivation and the strength to shake their hands and express sympathy. His father, the only member of his family whom I had seen once, was probably long gone. None of the other members of the family knew of me; I was of peripheral importance to their lives. I reasoned that an expression of sympathy from a total stranger would be soon cast into obscurity and not remembered. Stupidly, I thought, how lucky that I packed my black suit and a black silk blouse…But my appearance was totally irrelevant. Nobody paid any attention to me.

Among the sea of relatives a familiar person suddenly appeared, and I recognized Scott Tessier. With him were three young women in their late twenties, whose similar features and equally long, curly dark hair suggested that they were sisters. They spoke in turn about Will as a devoted, caring father. They were his nieces whom he had adopted when they were small children after their mother, Will's sister Olivia, and her husband had died in a car crash during a trip to Europe. I knew about his sister Olivia; Will had talked about her. But when we knew each other, she probably hadn't been married yet, her daughters not yet born.

Standing at the front of the room, Scott introduced the young women to the mourners. The two older ones, Tara and Tamara, were obviously twins, and the third one was their younger sister Tonia. Scott seemed incongruous in the tableau with his graying blond hair, receding hairline, and glasses. His jacket was open, showing a belly that protruded considerably over his tight waistline.

Tara spoke about a father who always listened patiently to her, the best father anyone could have. Tamara told us through tears of how he liked making pizza and that they were the best in the world. Tonia remembered how he encouraged her to pursue photography, and I later learned that she had had already quite a few sold-out exhibitions.

The young women spoke of a happy family, although somewhat unorthodox, with two fathers, Will and Scott, who alternately served as both mother and father when the girls were growing up. Tara and Tamara stood next to each other, with identical broken expressions on their identical oval faces, forcing their identical wide mouths into identical shy smiles. They were tall and skinny and stood awkwardly, bodies close together in mutual support. They were dressed alike, in layers of white and black tops with white scarves draped fashionably around their long necks, snuggly fitting black jeans, and black ballerina flats.

Tonia was a bit shorter than her twin sisters. She'd pulled her long dark hair into a loose ponytail, the end of which curved over her right shoulder. She wore similar layered tops of beige and black and a long beige scarf and identical snuggly fitting black jeans. But she wore high heels that made her almost as tall as her sisters. Everything about her was a softer version of her sisters, but I saw no resemblance in any of them to Will, their uncle, their adopted father. Tonia, the curvier, wispier, more elegant version of her twin sisters, spoke with a sure, confident voice at first, but then she burst into tears, unable to contain her misery and pain for having lost the "very best father anyone could have." After a pause she continued, presenting a picture of an ideal father, a talented artist, a man who in his extraordinary rich and active life found time for his children. I later learned that the girls had been adopted when Tara and Tamara were three years old. Tonia had been a baby and remembered no other parents but Will and Scott.

Utterly stunned, I needed a long time to process this new information, this secret life of Will's. A happy family of which I had no knowledge. The newspapers were brimming with Will's obituaries. From them I learned more about his life. About the life we did not share. Suddenly there was so much more to grieve.

I remembered Scott from our university days and how Will once introduced me to Scott's girlfriend Caroline, whom I now learned was actually Scott's younger sister. Why the deceit? But those were different days and being gay was not socially acceptable. But I was sure that Scott had known about Will and me. How had Will explained me to Scott? Had there been a fight, followed by make-up sex? Had they been attracted to each other from the very beginning, or had their closeness evolved after I had gone to Venezuela? Were they both bisexual in the beginning with a "fluid" sex drive? Adopting the girls probably had been a fortuitous move that legitimized their shared household. And in California it was easier to live a gay life.

In an absurdly detached way, I rationalized Will's life in California as a good reason for him never to have attempted to contact me. I could have contributed little to that life. Again, there was a stab of the residual regret of having been pushed out of his life. The loss was magnified by the realization that it was entirely mine.

The flight back to New York was again uneventful. I slept part of the way, seated in the middle seat between two overweight people, one of whom kept snoring and waking up, changing his position because he was unable to get comfortable, thus making me uncomfortable. Deeply unhappy and frustrated, I resented the bright and sun-drenched Los Angeles I had left. I wished it had rained. I wished people did not laugh at jokes and talk loudly. I wished the world would mourn with me.

At first I read the obituaries about Will with an unprecedented hunger for details about him, a craving for the minutiae of his everyday life that had been kept from me. I had this enormous need to know and be part of it all, even through this secondary, peripheral means. I rediscovered Will's website. His cinematic opus was chronologically listed and described in Wikipedia. How did I not know about all this? How did it all pass me by? I read all the available interviews with Will in magazines and ordered DVDs of his films, and of some educational videos, a series of lectures on film art and psychology. I watched them over and over, trying to find the younger version of Will, my Will, in the face of the narrator who now sported longer hair and an even more expressive face, carved and lined, making him appear wiser and more mature. On the whole his performance was familiar, though he had added to his lecturing repertoire a few expansive gestures with his hands, as if he were Italian and needed support of his hands in any dialogue. In the more recent videos of his lectures he moved with caution, a bit clumsily, not exactly ill at ease or uncomfortable, but awkwardly, as if it pained him to walk. His hair was longer but still dark without a single gray hair. I wondered, a bit maliciously, if it was dyed.

Suddenly there was—rage!

In vain I tried to convince myself that I was fine. But I was not fine. Who could I have been were it not for Will's rejection and betrayal? Carlos emerged as a victim too. Our marriage, as imperfect as it had been, was a victim, yet another piece of collateral damage. The abortion, which I now regretted with immense strength, became a gross error in judgment. My health, another piece of collateral damage. Siblings for Jason ... A larger family ... A more stable family for Jason.

My aspirations and dreams had all collapsed because of his rejection. My life had been derailed from its expected safe course. What course would it have taken had it not been stopped and overturned? What path had I not taken? What footprints in the sand had dissolved before they had had a chance to form? Who would I have become with him at my side? Would I have been a better, more likable, more accomplished person? What talents might have surfaced? What ideas never had a chance? What gifts had I denied Jason? What compassion had I failed to offer Carlos because of that frozen ten-year pause of my life? Would I have become a journalist, or even a filmmaker with Will's support? What if I had used the energy to create instead of in simply surviving? What if I could have left Carlos—how would my life be different? I had survived, but at what cost? What had I lost in the process? Was I a different person from the one I could have been?

Not knowing makes me sad and impotent at first, and then there is this incandescent, imploding rage, turned inward. It is too late to change what was. I am wistful for the person I could have been. With Will at my side, I am sure I would have been someone different. Not this ordinary aging person with a wrinkled face and graying hair and meager accomplishments. Should I be proud of just surviving a loss? Isn't there more to life? I realize that it is not regret for a future void, but rage for not having been given the opportunity to try, the opportunity to create freely without having to fight stubbornly for a balance. That's how it felt. It was a constant effort to retain an identity. Having to care for Jason helped a lot, because it took my mind off the penetrating despair and sadness and gave me courage to take the next step forward.

But today Jason is a grown man. Today I can let myself fully experience this overwhelming anger. Dismissing all objectivity, I direct it all at Will and Carlos. Will is to blame. Carlos is to blame. I had no choice. It is ridiculous to maintain that we always have a choice. These two men made decisions for me, constrained my actions, diminished me. They robbed me of my thirties. They robbed me of my dignity, my self-respect. Sequestered within the impoverished life their decisions created, I felt powerless. I really had no choice.

The world suddenly turns into a gargantuan regret. I wish I could live my life all over again, all of it, except for Jason. There seems too little of life remaining to support a drastic change. This realization of it all being in vain defeats me. I wait in silence after the deafening crush of lost ambitions, a silence that is a lie, devoid of direction and intent. I am alone on a subway platform, watching the fading lights of the train that has just left and which I missed.

I look at the sarcophagus box containing Will's letters. I take one out, start reading, and feel the newly surging rage. I tear it. After the first one the second is easier, and I keep shredding the letters into a pile at my feet, one after the other, until my fingers hurt and I search for scissors to make the job easier. The letters ... The letters started all this. They must be destroyed. But the rage does not ebb. I start hurling objects—pillows from the sofa, the Venetian glass bowl on the coffee table—and overturn chairs on the way to the kitchen.

I open kitchen cabinets and start throwing plates. First the ones on the lowest shelf, the ones I use every day; then the white Rosenthal plates; the long-stemmed wineglasses; the sturdier water glasses; the glass bowls—they create a satisfyingly jingling sound of broken glass—the ceramic bowls. I pick up anything that does not break and hurl it against the wall. I sit down exhausted on the floor. It is not very comfortable, although at first I do not notice. Only after a time, sitting on the shards of pottery, my back and my legs start to hurt. Exhausted, I pick myself up with much effort and slowly—oh, so slowly—creep into bed.

Awoken by a headache, a dry mouth, and a persistent need to urinate, I drag myself into the bathroom. After I wash my face, the headache remains. I look for aspirin only to find a bottle of baby aspirin, good for preventing cardiac problems but utterly inappropriate for this headache. I calculate, take four. Still with a headache, I resist, defer the look at the chaos in the living room and the kitchen: the broken wineglasses, broken china, the white Rosenthal plates that Carlos and I bought on our honeymoon in

Bermuda, and the ugly teapot that an aunt of Carlos's gave us. I had hated the tea set of Lenox china with dainty violets and had complained to Carlos that the teapot looked like a pregnant cow. We settled on the white, unadorned, minimalist Rosenthal china.

An hour passes. I now contemplate the damage on the floor with a mix of curiosity and incomprehension. I examine the pieces of broken glass and broken china, puzzled. I look with amazement at the broken chairs. Where did I find the strength to do that? How idiotic, such unproductive, unconstructive rage!

I sit in the dark so that those infinitesimally small particles of love will not have a chance to survive and will become trivial, unimportant. No! I turn on the light. "Let it be light" better serves this purpose. The light will eclipse the painful love remnants, bleach and sanitize them, render them nil, safe.

Among the chaos and detritus, I pick up my pocketbook with spilled credit cards and wonder, *Do I have enough credit to replace the china? The chairs? The wineglasses? All that is still broken in my life? Can I replace the irreplaceable and set my life straight? Do I have enough credit, enough value, enough leverage? Is there enough of a reserve left?*

Yes! With restored determination I pledge to replace what was broken, but the letters, Will's letters, are best destroyed. I pledge to accept the past and cradle it gently, cautiously, within my letter-less present. Imagining the living room pristine again, the contents of the kitchen cabinets replenished, and a new vase on the coffee table, I feel unburdened. Suddenly thirsty, I take a drink of water and then wash my face again and comb my hair. Slowly, deliberately, I let my final uncluttered journey begin.

CPSIA information can be obtained at www.ICGtesting.com
Printed in the USA
LVOW12s1826040813

346211LV00001B/72/P

9 781475 987737